James Mg. Allan

Father Stirling

Vol. 1

SALZWASSER
VERLAG

James Mg. Allan

Father Stirling

Vol. 1

Reprint of the original, first published in 1864.

1st Edition 2022 | ISBN: 978-3-75259-375-4

Verlag (Publisher): Salzwasser Verlag GmbH, Zeilweg 44, 60439 Frankfurt, Deutschland
Vertretungsberechtigt (Authorized to represent): E. Roepke, Zeilweg 44, 60439 Frankfurt, Deutschland
Druck (Print): Books on Demand GmbH, In de Tarpen 42, 22848 Norderstedt, Deutschland

FATHER STIRLING.

A NOVEL.

IN TWO VOLUMES.

BY

JAMES McGRIGOR ALLAN,

AUTHOR OF

"Nobly False," "The Cost of a Coronet," "The Last Days of a Bachelor," "The Intellectual Severance of Men and Women," &c.

"The Crown of Marriage is the experience of the *parental* feelings. I doubt if the man who has not known these tender ties; not felt these overflowing emotions—the sentiment of universal brotherhood which they engender—can really possess that full and perfect development of the heart which is absolutely necessary to the due discharge of the priestly office. We are called *Fathers*; yet we are forbidden to know a father's feelings, as alone they can be known by actual experience."

BOOK III. CHAP. III.

VOL. I.

London:

1864.

CONTENTS OF VOL. I.

BOOK FIRST.

BOOK SECOND.

BOOK THIRD.

BOOK FOURTH.

FATHER STIRLING.

BOOK I.

CHAPTER I.

THE ELOQUENT PRIEST.

Some five and twenty years since, one Sunday morning, in London, a large congregation had assembled in a church of the Romish persuasion. An ordinary spectator would have been struck with the vastness of the crowd, which not only filled the spacious building, but thronged the door-ways and knelt reverently in the streets. From the air of expectation which pervaded the multitude before the services began, it was evident that some unusual attraction had drawn them together. At length the grand music of the choir burst forth, the procession of priests and acolyths—carrying the cross, and clad in dresses glittering with gold, and white vestments—swept through the aisles of the edifice, and the imposing ritual of the Romish Church began.

Whatever may be our theological opinions, no one surely, with ordinary intelligence and perception of the beautiful, can witness unmoved, the celebration of High Mass. The very language in which the service is conducted—the language of our Roman conquerors and civilizers, and (until within the last two hundred years) the prevailing language of science throughout Europe; the language in which the treasures of classical literature have descended to, and are read by us, impresses the hearer by its numerous and vivid associations. Then, the number of ceremonial observances performed silently, carries the mind of the thinking spectator back to the time of the early christians, when persecution rendered these mute religious ceremonies absolutely necessary, and thus brings vividly before him the great age of this time-honoured worship. The Catholic Church appears to aim at touching the human heart, seemingly indifferent to the medium by which feelings of piety and veneration are excited—whether by preaching, music, pictures, or images. She enlists the whole of man's genius in the several departments of painting, architecture, sculpture, music, and eloquence; she unites all in her service, not in the vain idea that the creature can offer anything sufficiently worthy to the Creator, but that through the ministry of these arts, the human soul may be exalted from its ordinary condition, and elevated to the worship of God.

Special attention seemed to be directed to the officiating priest, and as the time approached for the pulpit to be occupied, it was whispered that this person was to preach his first sermon to a metropolitan congregation. When the reader calls to mind that the Mass is always said fasting, this fact might account for a great deal of the interest displayed in the man, but not altogether; his reputation as an eloquent preacher had preceded him, and it was this which had caused the unusually large congregation. All eyes were fixed on Father Stirling as he ascended slowly the winding stairs which led to the pulpit, affixed (as it frequently is in Romish churches) to one of the pillars. He was a man somewhat above the middle size, with dark brown hair and blue eyes. His body was spare, and his features thin almost to emaciation. Nevertheless his great natural beauty was rather enhanced than diminished by these peculiarities, which impressed his physiognomy with a rare expression of unworldliness, such as Raphael or Guido would have chosen for a Saint. His austerities gave him the appearance of being five years older than he really was. He looked three and thirty, but was only twenty-eight.

Such was the man, who, with hair closely cropped around his well-developed brows, and robed in the vestments of a parish priest, ascended with rather slow and tottering steps the pulpit stairs. It was quite evident he suffered from physical weakness, and this enhanced the impression which his comely and clerical appearance had already created. Especially the women showed in their countenances the compassion and sympathy which Father Stirling had created in their hearts. A keen observer might have noticed in the countenance and manner of the young priest other symptoms than those of physical debility. About for the first time to address a large metropolitan congregation, whose curiosity and expectation were highly excited, it was only natural that this man, abruptly called from his country parish, where he had ministered five years, should be oppressed with his insignificance and humility.

It was under the influence of these feelings that Father Stirling, in opposition to the wishes of his friends and other ecclesiastics, had gained his point and said Mass that morning.

Although a Catholic priest holding the belief that God is immanent in the Church, and firmly believing that the Spirit of Truth would speak through his lips, yet the *man* felt uneasy and alarmed at the trial to which he was to be submitted. Some men of a more practical turn of mind would have taken every earthly precaution to insure that which all preachers of every church and every denomination covet—a pulpit success!—they would carefully have prepared their sermons, either written them out or committed them to memory, and they would have taken pains to fortify their physical strength by an excellent breakfast. I am certain that celebrated west-end orator, the Honble. and Rev. Wycherley Winsome, would not have neglected the latter essential. He has been known to fortify himself by a cordial in the vestry before preaching. But Mr. Stirling was a young man, and not a man of this stamp. He was full of enthusiasm for the cause he had embraced. He attributed all his misgivings, so natural under the circumstances, to the weakness of his faith, to the sinfulness of the natural man, to the effect of Adam's fall; and in order to bring himself to the proper degree of holiness, he attended strictly to all his religious duties, and performed works of supererogation for some weeks previous to the ordeal. In particular he fasted, and on the eve of the important Sunday, still feeling nervous, he requested, and at length obtained permission of his ecclesiatical superior, to officiate in the celebration of the Mass.

From this the Rev. Mr. Stirling had been urgently dissuaded, and his diocesan had benevolently and warmly represented to him the extreme danger of reducing himself to such a degree of physical weakness, as might render him incapable of sustaining the excitement and the fatigue of preaching. Mr. Stirling, however, thought otherwise, and as zeal is never "snubbed" in the Romish Church, the good bishop at length, though somewhat reluctantly, gave his consent, perhaps vanquished by the representations of the young priest, that the spiritual strength afforded by partaking of the Holy Sacrament, would amply sustain his frail body and carry him victorious through the approaching trial.

This man, who had then for many weeks past only eaten the food barely necessary to support nature; who had drunk nothing stronger than water, had now eaten nothing since nine o'clock on the previous evening. He had been fifteen hours without food! No wonder that he tottered as he ascended the pulpit stairs! Throughout the whole of that morning, Father Stirling had been buoyed up by a species of holy inflation which he confidently believed to be the inspiration for which he pined. As the mass proceeded—as the deep tones of the organ rolled through the sacred edifice and alternated with trumpets, flutes, and piercing notes of the violins—as the rich voices of the male and female professional singers revelled in the glorious composition of Mozart, the priest was wrapt in a species of divine delirium.

The sublime music had its effect on his poetic nature ; he heard it not with that critical appreciation which characterized many a connoisseur present ; to him it sounded like a strain of heavenly melody, and suggested the idea of the song of the Herald Angels. Such is the wonderful effect of music on the strongly imaginative mind, well expressed by these words of Jean Paul Richter, "Away! away! thou speakest to me of things which in all my endless life I have found not, and shall not find!"

The effect of sacred music is to connect us more directly with the Infinite than any of the other arts. When the mystic rite which Protestants hold to be typical of, but which Catholics believe to be in itself the sacrifice of the Redeemer, had terminated, and when the sad and solemn strains of music were exchanged for a triumphant burst of jubilant harmony, the countenance of Father Stirling was radiant, like that of a man who doubts not of salvation.*

In this exalted frame of mind he entered the pulpit. Such was the strange mixture of spiritual strength and bodily weakness; the sunken eye burned brightly under the overhanging brow; the eagle-glance told of a prophet's and (if necessary) a martyr's cou-

* Music of the Mass: "Palestrina was impressed with the conviction that it was an experiment upon which, so to speak, depended the life and death of that grand description of music employed in masses. He proceeded to his task, with a conscious effort; and the words, 'Lord, enlighten mine eyes,' have been found in his manuscript. He did not succeed at once, his first two attempts having proved failures, but at length he brought to a bearing, in happy moments, the mass which is known by the name of Pope Marcellus' Mass, and in which he exceeded all expectations. It is full of simple melody, and yet, in point of variety, will stand a comparison with earlier masses; choruses separate and unite again; the meaning of the text is exquisitely brought out; the Kyrie is all prostration; the Agnus, humility; the Credo, majesty. Pope Pius IV., before whom it was executed, was in ecstacy. He compared it with heavenly melodies, such as those that the apostle John might have heard, when he was entranced. By this one great example the question was now for ever set at rest; a way was opened by which musical pieces have been produced, most beautiful in themselves, and most affecting even to persons of another faith. Who can hear them without being enwrapt? It is as if nature were endowed with music and a voice, as if the elements spoke, and all living things had united in one spontaneous concert of prayer; now rising and falling like the ocean, now darting up to heaven in one general shout of joy."—Ranke's Popes of Rome.

rage; but the cheek, save with the exception of one faint hectic tinge, was ghastly pale, and such was Father Stirling's weakness that he was obliged to hold mechanically by the stair-case rails as he ascended to the pulpit. An immense sea of upturned faces was before him. A low and significant murmur was succeeded by a perfect stillnesss. For an instant the priest felt abashed at the thought of his youth and inexperience, and that he was expected to instruct and edify so vast a number of his fellow-beings, among whom were so many wiser, older, and (as he believed) better than himself. But he banished this reflection by an effort of his will, as he remembered that he stood there, not as a man, but as an ambassador from God. His voice faltered a little as he gave out the text; but this disappeared as he proceeded with his subject.

He had been in the habit of preaching extemporaneously. On this occasion he had prepared notes, to which, however, he did not refer. He spoke from his heart right onwards.

He was unconscious of any effort. His physical weakness seemed to disappear. He felt sustained by some invisible power which he believed to be the direct co-operation of the Spirit of Truth. His voice filled the whole of the spacious church. His style displayed the graces of an experienced pulpit orator. All the charms of diction, metaphors, syllogisms, aphorisms, images of beauty, such as the composer of an elaborate discourse frequently seeks in vain to combine with effect, were showered forth with a profusion which seemed reckless, from the lips of the eloquent speaker; who felt, by that strange freemasonry which establishes the relation between preacher and congregation, that he carried his audience along with him. The intense silence was broken only by the sound of one voice, and those faint indescribable noises which characterize a large assemblage of persons listening attentively, and which occurred periodically when the preacher paused at the end of a paragraph.

The sermon was not argumentative or strictly in accordance with logical rules; and (read subsequently, as it was taken down by a skilful short-hand writer) it probably by no means satisfied its author's critical taste. It was exhortative, and might perhaps, when submitted to strict censorship, have illustrated the well-known reply of the Athenian orator to his client, when the latter complained that his defence on the third reading seemed no defence at all. "You forgot that the judges will only hear it once." Like the generality of effective sermons, it owed its special force to its delivery, and not a little to the peculiar circumstances under which it was delivered—the earnest manner, the pallid looks, the emaciated body of the priest, who, wrapt in his subject as he was, could not remain altogether unconscious of the prodigious effect he was producing.

As he approached the climax, his own feelings became wrought up and operated a sympathetic influence upon his hearers.

Appealing to each individual's state of self-examination, and his account with his own conscience, the preacher paused abruptly in the midst of a sentence. This, which with many preachers is a trick of stage-effect, not unfrequently learnt from an actor, was in this instance real and unpremeditated, and consequently produced a proportionate result. The orator was evidently overpowered with the magnitude of the question he had proposed; his abrupt and prolonged silence was more eloquent than words. The congregation, who had been gazing at him as the fascinated bird gazes on the serpent, showed signs of uneasiness—some moved excitedly in their seats—women had evidently great difficulty in controlling their emotions, and one lady fainted.

By a quick turn of thought the preacher calmed the agitation he had awakened, by reminding his hearers of the infinite mercy of God.

"You are helpless, forlorn, lost sinners—unable to work out your own salvation. I defy you to exert the free agency requisite to such a stupendous victory as to save your own souls. You are in despair, as you see opening before your eyes the gulf of eternal damnation." On this frightful picture he permitted the imagination to dwell for a time, and then abruptly thundered forth the words —"You would be saved? Lean then on the Saviour. Believe and live. He knows all your weakness, for He was himself a man. Only accept the sacrifice of His blood. You will do so—then, 'Though your sins be as scarlet, they shall be white as snow; though they be red like crimson, they shall be as wool.' Penitent sinners, who have believed in the Lord and accepted his conditions of mercy, tremble no more. Do you not hear? you are saved—saved—saved!" And he rushed into a description of the bliss awaiting the true believer in Paradise.

The sudden change from the awful idea of eternal perdition to eternal salvation was too much for the stoicism of the congregation.

The preacher concluded his discourse amid sounds which gave unmistakable evidence of awakened consciences and overflowing hearts. Strong men bent down their heads to conceal their emotion. Women sobbed audibly. But the excitement and the physical fatigue following on long abstinence at length produced their effect. Exhausted nature succumbed before the labours imposed by the ardent and indefatigable spirit. As he brought his address to a conclusion, and before he had time to pronounce the benediction—the priest's voice failed him—his eyes swam—he reeled and fell in the pulpit.

CHAPTER II.

THE JESUIT TUTOR.

CLEMENT STIRLING, whom I have thus introduced to my readers, and whose history forms the chief part of the contents of the following pages, was the son of a gentleman of moderate but independent fortune, who lived in ——shire, England. Mr. Stirling, a strict member of the Church of England, and holding the tenets of the Evangelical party, married a lady of the Romish persuasion, and it had been expressly stipulated in the marriage contract, that, of the children which might result from their union, the boys should be educated in their father's, the girls in their mother's persuasion. Clement Stirling was the only child whom they succeeded in rear-ing to manhood. Mrs. Stirling, who was deeply grieved that no girl had survived, evinced a very ardent desire to infringe the agreement, but as Mr. Stirling was firm, she was compelled reluctantly to submit to see her only child educated in the Protestant religion; which, according to her narrow and bigoted views, was equivalent to consigning him to everlasting perdition.

The reader must bear in mind that the Romish and Anglican creeds mutually declare their respective churches the only true religion, out of whose pale no one can be saved. It is, however, only the fanatical and the ignorant of both persuasions who really believe this. The liberal and enlightened are happily much better than their creeds would make them.

When Clement was sixteen his father died suddenly from the effects of a fall while hunting, and this event changed the whole course of his education and future destiny. His mother immediately threw off all pretence of adhering to the solemn promise she had made to her late husband. Yet she had loved her husband, and with this sole exception had proved herself a good wife. But what can withstand religious fanaticism? Not even her affection for her husband's memory, not even her knowledge of his last wishes, could compete with what she regarded as an infinitely higher duty, affecting her conscience and the eternal welfare of her son.

This woman doubtless meant well, but was totally unfit for the sole discharge of so grave a responsibility as the moral, mental, and religious culture of her children. She belonged to that class of women who illustrate the truth of Pope's lines—

> "A little learning is a dangerous thing;
> Drink deep, or taste not, of the Pierian spring."

Such, on the strength of a smattering of superficial knowledge, think themselves in every respect the intellectual equals of men; and by their pitiful mania for having their own way, and gratifying the feminine passion of ruling, and carrying out the little short-sighted projects of the moment, are almost certain—if uncontrolled—to injure irreparably the welfare of those whom they most love.

Although Mrs. Stirling consulted the opinion of the world so far as to leave her son at liberty to attend the Anglican Church, and outwardly to appear a Protestant, she did her utmost to convert him in secret to the profession of her own faith. His previous tutor, a clergyman of the Establishment, was dismissed, and in his place was substituted the Rev. Mr. Wiley, a Romish ecclesiastic. This gentleman, who had been educated at Paris, was about seven and twenty, and to considerable learning and accomplishments united the ease and polished manner of a man of the world. He spoke French as fluently as his native tongue, which was English, and in short presented an excellent specimen of that remarkable compound of the lay and clerical characters—the French *Abbé*.

In selecting such a person to complete her son's education, Mrs. Stirling showed considerable judgment. She doubtless foresaw that to the ascendancy exerted by Mr. Wiley's professional capacity, scholastic attainments, and knowledge of the world, would be added the influence of a travelled and agreeable man young enough to gain the confidence of his pupil. Events justified these anticipations. Mr. Wiley made himself more a companion than a tutor, and soon succeeded in gaining Clement's affections. Having won the boy's heart he proceeded carefully to lay siege to his understanding. And in this undertaking he showed his consummate knowledge of human nature.

Had Mr. Wiley attempted at once to convert Clement from the Protestant to the Romish faith by argument, he would have met with stout opposition, but his tact taught him to avoid this blunder. He did not appeal directly to the boy's mind or judgment, but to that which at his age and in this particular instance was far more susceptible—the imagination. Mrs. Stirling had begun to tamper with her son's religious impressions while quite a child. She had frequently persuaded him to be present at the saying of Mass, and at other devotions in a little oratory which by her husband's permission had been fitted up for her use, on the express understanding that Clement was never to enter it. It is needless to say the boy had been expressly charged to keep these visits a secret from his father. There is to the youthful mind—and to the adult also—something expressly attractive in that which is furtive and forbidden. Was it not Madame de Montespan—or at any rate one of The Most Christian King's mistresses—who, when ordered by her physician to drink a glass of cold water, exclaimed—"Oh that this were a sin that it might become agreeable!"

Clement tasted a fearful joy on these occasions. He loved his mother, and though his conscience hinted that she was doing wrong, he thought it would be dishonourable to betray her to his father. Little did Mrs. Stirling suspect the future she was preparing for her son by thus tampering with his faith and conscience. Thus he was sufficiently prepared by these and other means to be deeply impressed by the spectacle of High Mass, witnessed for the first time after his father's death, in the Romish Church of the county town, and accompanied by Mrs. Stirling and Mr. Wiley.

I have already touched on the august ceremonies of the Romish Ritual, and their effect on the mind of a boy of sixteen may be imagined, especially when it is recollected that the spectator had a cultivated mind and an ardent imagination. It is, I think, a great mistake to suppose that the worship of the Romish Church has most effect on the ignorant and unrefined. This event formed an era in the boy's life. He saw everything magnified and enriched with fabulous hues through the prism of his imagination, which had been dangerously developed at the expense of the immature judgment. He was impressed by the provincial chapel as though it had been a gorgeous medieval cathedral; literally and morally dazzled by the lighted tapers, the rich dresses of the officiating priests, the perfume from the censers, the grand altar-piece of the Crucifixion, which he thought the most wonderful piece of art he had ever seen, the various other pictures, representing scenes in the life of Christ, lastly the delicious—the entrancing music; everything in short appealed to the youth's susceptibilities, and touched his heart.

For the first time, as it seemed to him, had the reality of that great sacrifice been thoroughly brought home to him. That which had been hitherto rendered hackneyed from the lips of preachers—often dull, lukewarm, and indifferent—was now placed within the conception of the most ordinary intelligence as a great fact, by prayer and praise, without the utterance of a word from the pulpit. And when the little bell warned all devout Catholics to lower their heads at the elevation of the Host,* it flashed across the mind of Clement that the doctrine which our Catholic ancestors believed for centuries, (and which is still professed by a hundred and forty millions, more than twice the number of Protestants,) might, after all, be true. And when the wailing and plaintive music gave place to the ringing notes, so eloquently expressive of triumphant thanksgiving, at the completion and acceptation of the "sacrifice" of the mass, Clement, if he did not actually believe, was far advanced towards the belief of those around him.

The imagination and the heart were captivated. The judgment slept. Then and there Clement Stirling may have been said to become a proselyte to Rome. A significant look passed between his mother and Mr. Wiley. Having effected a moral conquest, Mr. Wiley

* A.D. 1230 Gregory added the little bell to inform people when to kneel down to adore the Host.—
Novelties of Romanism, by C. H. COLLETTE.

gradually had recourse to theological discussion with his pupil. I will not dwell on the controversial weapons he employed. They may easily be imagined; and I have no desire to convert this work into a polemical treatise. Clement battled more for the sake of his pride than any other reason; in reality wishing to be convinced. He felt it was no disgrace to be vanquished in argument by such superior abilities as Mr. Wiley possessed, who, when he judged it advisable, brought forth all his strength and hid the weak points of his cause under a cloud of eloquence and appeal to the feelings, which Clement found irresistible. The Romish ecclesiastic painted the venerable church which had borne the brunt of angry embittered opposition, which had rescued letters from destruction, which had been the bulwark and encourager of literature and art, the preserver of classic records; which had, in short, so ably played her part in civilizing Europe. Some ugly facts connected with the beginning of the reformation and the history of some of the popes, Mr. Wiley did not dwell upon. He passed, in the most cursory manner, over the faults and blots in the Church of Rome. He set all her beauties in the fairest light, and certainly gave a grand and glowing description of that church which has fastened her roots so deeply in the affections of men, and which, in the belief of some profound thinkers, is destined still to preserve her influence, to recover all her pristine supremacy, and to re-absorb all other religions into her capacious bosom.

In short, Clement Stirling abjured the 'Great Heresy,' as Mr. Wiley denominated all Protestant creeds, and was re-baptized into the Church of Rome.

CHAPTER III.

THE ROMISH CONVERT.

CLEMENT STIRLING was eighteen when he became a convert to Rome. There were, however, stringent reasons why this change of religion should not be known beyond his own family. Clement was the heir to a considerable property, and it was thought advisable, both by Mrs. Stirling and Mr. Wiley, that the young man should still outwardly conform to the established religion, lest the executors of his father's will might raise some difficulties respecting the legality of the inheritance. During the life-time of his father, a romantic attachment had grown up between Clement and a young lady of great beauty and accomplishments — Miss

Madeline Singleton, only daughter of a retired Colonel. The late Mr. Stirling and Colonel Singleton, whose views on politics and religion coincided, had been intimate friends. Their respective properties joined. They had seen with approval the intimacy growing up between their children, and given their sanction to a union at a fitting period.

The impulse which urged Clement to make Madeline acquainted with the change in his religious sentiments, was checked by his mother, and Clement was reluctantly persuaded to appear a Protestant, both to the world, and in the eyes of her whom he loved, at least till his arrival at his twenty-first year put him in possession of his estate; which duly took place without the executors of the will having any idea of his change of religious sentiments. It had been intended to solemnize the marriage at this period, but from various causes it was delayed a year. About three months before the time fixed for this interesting event, Mr. Wiley, who had all along affected the deepest interest in Miss Singleton, one day when Clement was, lover-like, dwelling on her merits, took the occasion to say :—

"But is not Miss Singleton a very strict Protestant ?"

"Of course she is," replied Clement, with some surprise. "You must be quite as well aware of the fact as myself."

"You have never even hinted at the change in your views ? She still believes you to be a member of her own Church ?"

"Certainly," replied Clement. "Till I came of age, you know, both you and my mother thought it might prejudice my interests to make the fact known."

"But since," said Mr. Wiley "I have not advised you to keep the secret since."

This was strictly true. Mr. Wiley had not spoken upon the subject at all, but Clement construed his silence into approval of his conduct, of which he had often informed his tutor, from whom indeed he had no secrets.

"Why," said Clement, with some hesitation, "knowing the strictness of Colonel Singleton's views on religion, I thought it best not to say anything. In this my own opinion and my mother's agree."

"You really think," said Mr. Wiley, "that her father would object to her marrying you if he knew you belonged to the Church—that you had abjured the Anglican heresy?"

"I am convinced of it," replied the young man. "But as I am to be Madeline's protector for the future, I conceive myself to be the best judge on that point; and I do not doubt that after marriage she will in due time embrace the religion of her husband."

"I would not be too sure of that," said Mr. Wiley. "I have paid considerable attention to Miss Singleton's physiognomy and conversation, and my impression is that she is not in this respect like the ordinary run of women, who submit to be dictated to by their male relatives on social, moral, and religious questions."

Clement replied earnestly. "You surely cannot conceive me capable of attempting to dictate to Madeline what she is to believe. Oh, no! I hope to convince my wife by time and patience that she is in the wrong. I should despise any woman who should at once profess to agree with me on such an all-important question; that would be hypocrisy or indifference—and Madeline is incapable of either."

"But suppose," persevered Mr. Wiley, "that in spite of all your efforts, your wife should still persist in adhering to the religion of her fathers—the faith which she learned in childhood, and which is associated with all her freshest and most hallowed feelings. You must remember, my dear Clement, that women are not like men in this respect; they do not reason, they only feel; thus they are extremely positive because they do not possess the mental calibre necessary to understand appeals to the intellect; and the most sensible women have a glimmering of their deficiency. They have a misgiving of their own mental inferiority, and so guard themselves by utterly refusing and ignoring argument."

Clement was too much disconcerted by the magnitude of the question at issue, to notice the inconsistency of Mr. Wiley's remarks in adducing at the same time, Miss Singleton's mental strength and weakness, as opposing agencies to her being open to conviction. He endeavoured to turn the conversation, by saying with an affectation of indifference which he was far from feeling:

"Well, then, should Madeline be unwilling to change her worship, we must make a compact like that made by my own parents."

Mr. Wiley did not care to remind Clement, how completely his mother had violated her part of the compact. It might have given rise to some awkward reflections. He only said:

"Have you never thought of the other alternative—that Miss Singleton might possibly pervert you?"

Clement laughed, for, like all young men, he was a great believer in himself.

"What!" he said, "a woman, who, according to your own showing, does not possess the mental calibre requisite to understand appeals to reason—such a one shake the sincere and deliberate convictions of an educated man!"

Doubtless Mr. Wiley laughed inwardly, but he preserved his outward gravity as he said:

"But when that woman is your wife—when she exerts the daily, hourly influence of her beauty, her accomplishments, her *love*—those thousand means of seduction which women possess over our sex—"

Even Clement, in spite of his infatuation, was struck with the unclerical tone of this speech, and as he regarded his ex-tutor and present friend and adviser earnestly, could not help saying, with the frankness of youth:

"But, Mr. Wiley, what can you, a priest, know of the seductions of women?"

Mr. Wiley was never confused, and never without his answer. He smiled as he replied in his most gracious manner:

"That is a home-thrust, my dear Clement, to which I reply—personally, and from my own knowledge, I grant you—nothing! but in my professional capacity I am forced to learn much of which I would rather remain ignorant. Then, one cannot go through the world with one's eyes and ears shut, and how much is to be learned from reading! Directly and individually, the sex is to me a sealed book. As a priest, I can never know a woman's love for me; but all history, sacred as well as profane, is so explicit as to female character, that even a recluse like myself cannot profess entire ignorance. But to return to the subject, as your old instructor, guardian, and friend, as one standing, in intention, at least, *in loco parentis*, having a lively regard for your temporal as well as your eternal welfare, I did indeed advise you to keep the change in your religion a secret, until you had arrived at man's estate, for many obvious reasons, which it would be tedious and superfluous to recapitulate. Now, the matter assumes a totally different aspect; you are about to marry a young, beautiful, and accomplished woman; is it right, just, or honourable, to keep her in the dark on so momentous a question?"

Clement was silent—a prey to contending emotions. His conscience told him Mr. Wiley was in the right; but why had he not said this before? why had he not advised him to take Madeline into his confidence, immediately on completing his twenty-first year? He attributed Mr. Wiley's previous silence to delicacy—to a dislike to seem officious.

Mr. Wiley seemed to read his thoughts, for he said:

"You think I should have said this before. Perhaps I should; but I thought it better to leave the decision entirely to yourself, as you had arrived at years of discretion; and I only speak now because, the marriage is drawing near, and I should not like to see you lay yourself open to a charge of having deviated from the path of honourable dealing. You dread making your intended wife acquainted with the fact that you have joined the Catholic Church lest it might result in cancelling your engagement. Surely, surely, her father cannot be so intolerant. She loves you; you have been betrothed for years; will not her love stand this test? Rest assured that she will only think more highly of you than ever. And should her father prove intractable at first, trust to her own affection. When she is legally her own mistress, she will doubtless decide for herself, even in spite of her father's prohibition."

Little did Clement Stirling imagine the perfidy concealed under this plausible advice, that Mr. Wiley was actually in league with Mrs. Stirling to cancel the engagement with Madeline. Mrs. Stirling, not wishing her son to marry a Protestant, had never favoured the match; and Mr. Wiley was actuated by secret motives which will be disclosed in due time.

Thoroughly under the influence of Wiley, and believing him to be his best friend, Clement allowed himself to be persuaded to do at last, what he should have done immediately after joining the Romish faith. He determined to inform Miss Singleton that he was a Catholic. But how should the disclosure be made? After long deliberation, he sat down and wrote a letter, in which he broke the intelligence as gently and with as many precautions as possible. He gave, *in extenso*, his reasons for embracing the Romish faith, and also for concealing the fact so long. He concluded an elaborate, powerful, and affecting letter, by an eloquent appeal to her reason and her love, and said that, although he anticipated some objection from her father, he naturally trusted, as they both believed in the principal tenets of Christianity, the distinctions in their respective modes of worship would not sunder them.

Clement was mistaken; a long correspondence was the result, as well as several painful interviews, in which each tried, unsuccessfully, to convert the other. Thus passed three months. One day Madeline was dreadfully agitated; she explained that she felt guilty in carrying on this correspondence, and seeing Clement clandestinely. She had not dared to tell her father, well knowing what the consequences would be. But she could no longer keep the secret from him; he had questioned her as to the cause of her dejection, the inequality of her spirits, and when he found her in tears, which was often the case, insisted upon knowing the cause.

"Shall I tell him, Clement?" added the poor girl. "May I tell him? Oh, I cannot bear this load upon my conscience any longer."

Clement replied, in a tone of desperation—

"Tell him then, and let us know the worst."

On the following day, to his great astonishment, he received a very abrupt and angry letter from Colonel Singleton, stating that he must consider the engagement with Miss Singleton at an end; that all letters, tokens, &c., must be exchanged, and that further communication between the lovers must cease. At the same time, Clement received a package containing all the letters he had sent Madeline. This abrupt and unkind proceeding nearly prostrated the young man. Half-distracted with grief, he replied immediately to Colonel Singleton, refusing to believe that his daughter could be a willing party to this summary conduct; and that unless he heard it from her own lips, he could not believe that she would thus abruptly cancel her plighted faith on the score of difference in religious sentiments. He received a reply, as follows—

"Colonel Singleton begs to acknowledge Mr. Stirling's letter of the twelfth of November, in reply to his of the eleventh. The youth of Mr. Stirling, and the excitement under which he writes, are extenuating circumstances, which lead Colonel Singleton to overlook the implied charge of want of veracity in his statements made in the letter of the above date. Colonel Singleton has to repeat that he considers himself the best judge of the conditions necessary to secure his daughter's happiness. If Mr. Stirling thinks the Colonel's note abrupt, let him seek the sufficient cause in his (Mr. Stirling's), systematic deception of years, in hiding from the world, and more especially from those who had a right to his confidence, the change in his religion. Had Mr. Stirling chosen to pursue a more frank and honourable course, Colonel Singleton would have acted accordingly. Mr. Stirling has himself to thank for the 'abruptness' of which he complains. Nevertheless, as Colonel Singleton does not desire to model his conduct on that of his correspondent, if Mr. Stirling will call at twelve a.m. to-morrow, at Vittoria House, he will be convinced from Miss Singleton's own lips, that in cancelling the engagement, she is acting of her own free will."

CHAPTER IV.

A COLONEL OF THE OLD SCHOOL.

CLEMENT STIRLING was outwardly calm on the morrow, as he walked up the long avenue leading to Vittoria House. All that had passed seemed to him but a dream. Memory continually tempted him to forget the sad errand on which he was bent. It seemed so natural that he should be going, as he had often gone before to meet a welcome reception, and to forget the lapse of time, in the society of Madeline and her father. The gate-keeper touched his hat, as usual; Ponto, the house-dog, came bounding forward to meet him. There were no external signs of change—nothing, save the consciousness of the dead weight at his heart. He rang the bell; the door was opened, and Clement was ushered by the old servant into the drawing-room. In the midst of his grief Clement was keenly observant, and he fancied he could perceive something in the manner of this man (an old soldier, who had served the Colonel for many years), which betrayed some knowledge of the altered relation in which the visitor stood towards the family.

Colonel Singleton was standing before the fire in that peculiar attitude so much affected by middle-aged and elderly gentlemen. He was a tall man, with grey hair and moustache, dressed in a blue braided frock, Wellington boots, and black leather stock—in short, the complete dress of the period worn by a military man on half-pay. The Colonel's age was fifty-six; but his stalwart figure, his erect soldierly bearing made him appear a few years younger. His strongly-marked countenance was bronzed with oriental suns, for he had fought under Wellington in India, as well as in the Peninsula, and he wore on his breast the medals commemorating half-a-dozen pitched battles in which he had been engaged, as well as some foreign orders. The Colonel always wore these decorations on state occasions, and when he had to transact any business which he considered of particular importance. The expression of his features was that of stern determination and indomitable firmness of character. Long years of military service had taught him to consider implicit obedience to orders as one of the highest virtues. Accustomed to command, and to have his will accepted as law, this veteran had acquired a harsh, abrupt, imperious manner of speaking, and an impatience of contradiction. He was still morally at the head of his regiment. Nevertheless he was a gentleman, and not naturally hard-hearted.

He received Clement more kindly than might have been expected from the tone of his note. Doubtless the grief and anxiety so unmistakeably depicted on the young man's countenance, touched the old officer, for he said, as he motioned his visitor to a chair—

"Be seated, sir. Believe me, I regret sincerely this unfortunate change of religion, on your account as well as that of my daughter. You are the son of my old friend Maurice Stirling."

"You mistake if you imagined that I in any way reflected on your sincerity—" began Clement, who was too much agitated to finish the sentence.

"There is no occasion to refer to that, sir," said the Colonel. "The case simply stands thus: When I permitted Miss Singleton to contract an engagement with you, I did so under the firm impression that your father's intentions respecting you would be strictly carried out. I thought you were, and would remain, a Protestant. I was not prepared to find that your religious opinions had been tampered with."

Clement made a gesture of impatience and denial. The Colonel continued—

"I have no wish to offend you, young man, but I am a plain speaker, and I wish you perfectly to understand me. I discover suddenly that you have been for years a communicant of the Romish Church. I regret it for your sake sincerely; but that, of course, is your own affair. My duty is clear. You have for some time been carrying on a clandestine correspondence with my daughter, for the express purpose of perverting her to your own way of thinking. Have the goodness to hear me out, and then I will listen to you in turn. I repeat—of perverting her. Your letters I have read. I ordered my daughter to show them to me, and she, of course, obeyed. I only hope it is not yet too late to counteract the mischief this correspondence may have done. Your letters are clever; they evince your scholarship and logical skill. I wish your abilities had been enlisted in a better cause. Understand me, sir; as a strict member of the Church of England, the best sample of the reformed religion in the world, I hold the doctrines of that church whose head is the Bishop of Rome, to be damnable and heretical, and I am determined to have no more tampering with my daughter's faith.

"Now, sir, put yourself in my place, in a father's place, and tell me how could I have acted otherwise than I have done, and am now doing. Remember that you have dealt most unfairly in not avowing your change of opinion from the very first. If my letter appeared unnecessarily harsh and abrupt, you must ascribe it to my very natural indignation on making this discovery. Permit me to conclude; I have no wish to enter into your reasons for changing your religion. You are, of course, sincere. Your letters and conduct prove that; for you have everything to lose by becoming a Catholic."

"Except eternal life!" interrupted Clement Stirling.

"Well, sir," continued the Colonel, "that is your opinion. Enjoy it; I have no wish to enter into a theological controversy with you. I was about to say, when you interrupted me, that though your letters prove your sincerity, and although you have clothed your opinions in good language, that your arguments will not bear inspection. In fact, I consider them ridiculous. You are a very young man. I am nearly three times your age, and your father's old friend, and I will take this opportunity, as our paths in life diverge from this time, and we may never meet again, to say that you have, in my opinion, some very bad advisers. Your mother is *your mother!* She is wrong, but she is to be pardoned, to be loved in spite of the mischief she is doing you; but as for that Jesuit, that Father Wiley, beware of that man! He has a flattering insinuating manner, like all those fellows who have been bred in France, the land of insincerity,* but

* At the time of which I am writing, orthodox, moral and constitutional England could not forgive France the great Revolution. The *entente cordiale* did not exist, and Englishmen of Colonel Singleton's stamp heartily despised a national character which they did not in the least understand. How great a change in public opinion in this respect has taken place within thirty—nay, within ten years! It appears to me that France is better understood by England than England is understood by France.

he is a priest, and a Frenchman in everything but the name. There is something forbidding in his aspect, in spite of his soft, silky manner. He can't look you straight in the face. I never saw a popish priest who could. Depend upon it, he has some personal end in view in making you a proselyte, which you will discover when it is too late. Now, sir, in conclusion, at my daughter's request, I have permitted you to have one last interview with her alone. Young man," said the grim Colonel, relenting for a moment, "I did hope to have called you son. That can never be; but I trust to the honour of your father's son, and I am too well assured of the duty and affection of my daughter, to have any misgivings in permitting this. I will send Miss Singleton to you. Farewell, sir."

The Colonel marched towards the young man, pressed the hand which Clement mechanically held out, and left the room.

CHAPTER V.

THE CANCELLED ENGAGEMENT.

Clement Stirling sank on a chair, leant his elbows on a little table where he had often played chess with Madeline, and covered his face with his hands. So profoundly was the young man absorbed in his grief, that he did not notice the sound made by the opening and shutting of a door opposite to that by which Colonel Singleton had left the room. He was at length roused from his sad reverie by a sob from a person quite close to him. He looked up, and through his tears saw Madeline—a beautiful fair-haired, blue-eyed girl of seventeen—who stood weeping beside her lover. Clement exclaimed—

"O, Madeline, must it be? Must we sever? Is there no intermediate course?"

"None, none," replied the weeping girl. "It must be broken off at once. We—we must meet no more." Convulsive sobs stopped her utterance for a while.

"O, Clement," she continued, "why were you not more explicit at first? Why did you not tell me of the great change which had taken place in your religious convictions ere you had made me love you so? Then we might not have been so wretched, Clement; it was wrong, it was very, very wrong."

How could Clement Stirling justify himself? Her reproach was deserved, and besides it proved how much she loved him.

"But," he exclaimed, "is there no hope? May not your father be induced to show more toleration? We both believe in the same God. Why, because we worship Him somewhat differently, must we cancel the most sacred vows and render each other wretched?"

"Clement," replied Madeline, "my father

has forbidden me to marry you, and that is sufficient. Independently of his command being my law, he conversed with me seriously and kindly, and my own heart acknowledges the truth of his advice. It is impossible with such important differences of opinion between us that we could ever be to one another what man and wife ought to be. Ah! why embitter the last moments we shall ever pass together by recrimination and argument? Have you not already displayed your opinions at great length in your letters and in our previous interviews? I can never think as you do."

"Madeline," said Clement, abruptly, "you never loved me, or you could not make up your mind to separate from me so easily. In the Bible it is said that man and wife are one flesh, and a solemn engagement such as ours is almost equivalent to a marriage."

"Clement," replied Madeline, "I can forgive you this injustice, at this moment. If this is a time for reproaches, they certainly should not come from you."

"And such are women's vows, of which we hear so much!" said Clement bitterly. "You will forget me and marry another."

"Time will show whether I will do that," returned Madeline, in a resigned tone. "No, Clement, though it is you who have virtually caused the canceling of our engagement, and condemned me instead of the happy future I had so long anticipated, to a cheerless and solitary career, I will never cease to love and pray for you."

"Then—then," exclaimed Clement, softened by the angelic sweetness of her reply, "if you do love me so well as you say, and as I have always believed, why will you not make this sacrifice for me? What is love, if it does not comprehend a sacrifice like this? You should prefer me to your father. You should actually and practically put unreserved trust in the man whom you single out from all other men to become your husband. Religion gives the dominion to the man. It is expressly so declared in Scripture in these words, 'And thy desire shall be to thy husband and he shall rule over thee.' My faith should be your faith. You should mistrust your own judgment, your own convictions, your own opinions. You should sit at my feet and accept the truth from my lips—at least you should try to comprehend, to think, to believe as I do. This is what a loving woman would do. If you really loved me, this is what you would do for me. You would imitate the conduct, and paraphrase the words of the Moabitish woman to her mother-in-law:—'Intreat me not to leave thee, or to return from following after thee: for where thou goest I will go; and where thou lodgest I will lodge: thy people shall be my people, and thy God my God.'"

At these words Madeline wept bitterly. They conveyed a touching association of ideas, a cherished remembrance, quite independent of their own beauty. There was a choral society, of which Madeline was a member, in the county town. Medeline possessed a voice which would have been a fortune to a professional singer, and often had Clement Stirling listened enraptured to her splendid *recitativo* of the above words of Ruth to Naomi.

But Clement Stirling, a prey to remorse of conscience, and unable at that moment to exercise the magnanimity requisite to acknowledge his error, felt the necessity of having a victim. He was lashing himself into a fury, and went on—"We hear much of the great sacrifices women are willing to make for the men they love. I wish to believe, to have a proof of this. I ask you to perform your solemn vows. I do not ask you to profess a faith in which you do not believe. God forbid! All I ask, and this I have a right to expect, is that you should marry me in spite of our religious difference. Will you not trust yourself with me because I am a Catholic, because I have embraced from due conviction what was the faith of our English ancestors, till that monster Henry the Eighth quarrelled with the Pope about permission to divorce his wife; the faith of two-thirds of Christendom at the present day, the faith that is destined to survive all the attacks of heretics, and once more to unite all the nations of the earth in one covenant, in one fold, under one shepherd. But I give you my solemn word of honour that I will make no attempt to convert you. Have you no confidence in the man to whom you have been betrothed three years? I have already said that if we become *one*, I will make the same compact with you that my father made with my mother."

Here, Madeline's maid knocked at the door, and having obeyed her mistress's summons to enter, said:

"Please miss, the Colonel wishes to see you directly."

"Yes; say I am coming."

The servant left the room. Madeline cast her eyes upon a little *ormolu* clock on the mantel-piece. The time allotted by the Colonel had long expired. Their conversation, of which I have only reported a summary, had already lasted considerably over an hour.

"Once more, Clement, I beseech you, let us not waste the precious moments in useless recrimination. I will make every sacrifice for you that a good woman ought to make. I will sacrifice my life if necessary, but not my duty to my father, not my conscience, not the salvation of my soul. Do you not see that the scheme you propose is impracticable, that if we married you could not, even if you would, refrain from influencing my religious opinions; and—pardon me, Clement, for referring to it, —but has the compact made between your parents been fulfilled? Are not your present convictions and our cancelled engagement a proof to the contrary. Oh! do not misunderstand me. I say not this in reproach, but in kindness, in pity to both of us. And here, let me tell you, dear Clement, about to be separated as we are for ever, in this world, once for all, with no wish to offend, that I feel a deep conviction you have taken a wrong step in departing from the religion of your noble father. I hope you will repent and retrace it before the consequences are irrevocable. Now," she added, in tones which completely dismissed Clement's bitterness, "let us take a last farewell."

And she held up her beautiful face to receive the kiss which Clement placed upon her lips. Her eyes were swimming in tears—her face was deadly pale—her lips were cold. At this moment, the Colonel, whose patience was exhausted, entered the room. He was inclined to be angry, that the interview had been prolonged so far beyond the time which he had fixed; but the touching spectacle presented by these two young people loving each other so dearly, yet about to be severed for ever from conscientious motives, disarmed the old man's passion. He stood for some moments irresolute, doubtless recalling some reminiscence of his own youth.

"Madeline," he began, in a voice much more husky than usual. He stopped and blew his nose. The old veteran was ashamed of feelings which did him honour. He advanced just in time to support his daughter, who sank fainting in his arms, her fair head partially concealing some of the decorations which glittered on the old soldier's breast. He waved his hand, but not unkindly, as a signal for Clement to depart. The latter obeyed mechanically, moving like a man in a dream. He retained but an indistinct remembrance of what happened from the moment when Madeline sank fainting in her father's arms, to that in which he found himself walking briskly down the avenue from Vittoria House—with a horrible sensation of an aching void in his heart—which made the world seem to him at two-and-twenty, a vast "unweeded garden," a huge lonely wilderness—the grave of happiness and hope.

CHAPTER VI.

DRIFTING TOWARDS A FATAL RESOLUTION.

There are few experiences more bitter than the first crushing disappointment to our hopes in youth. If you take a bauble from a child, he cries, and men, these "children of a larger growth," are continually pursuing some object on which they have set their whole hearts, and disappointment in attaining this object, drives them to despair. But all disappointments in after life are as nothing compared with the sudden destruction of youthful illusions. A fit of illness, in which he might barely have escaped with life would, perhaps, have worked a moral cure in Clement Stirling. Instead of this violent remedy, however, the unfortunate young man sank into a fit of melancholy in which he would pass days without speaking. His mother feared for the reason of her son, and with justice. Clement's mind frequently wandered. He displayed no interest in any of his usual occupations, nor, indeed, in anything else. Study, exercise, all things were neglected, and when he betrayed any consciousness of his actual position, it was only to confirm his mother's gloomy forebodings, by stating his own firm conviction that he was going mad.

Eminent medical men were called in, but they could do nothing beyond advising change of scene, and every effort which could tend to excite the dormant energies of the mind, and give the patient an interest in life. If this could be done, if Clement could be induced to betray the slightest intellectual energy, time would do the rest, and the young man would be finally restored to the use of his noble mind. Clement was certainly in a very dangerous condition, for hitherto every effort on the part of his mother and Mr. Wiley had failed to rouse him. The latter, however, who had studied this peculiar form of mental disease, devoted himself with unremitting attention to the cure of his old pupil, and prevented the hopes of his mother from being quite extinguished. Whatever personal motives might have actuated Mr. Wiley, it was certainly owing to his instrumentality, that Clement eventually recovered the full use of his reason. For several weeks when his state of despondency was at the worst, Mr. Wiley never left Clement for an instant, and the young man subsequently acknowledged that he owed everything to this constant vigilance. When he awoke in the morning, instead of springing to his feet full of joy and life in the consciousness of youth, physical and mental strength, the unfortunate victim of hypochondria would lie in his bed, oppressed with vain terrors, imaginary fears, dreading to face the long day before him. Such was a specimen of the dreadful revelations of this critical period of his malady.

By taking advantage of every opportunity to soothe and calm his agitated mind; by conversing with him when he would speak; by reading to him when he would listen; and by sitting with him silently when he refused to do either, and thus giving him the consolation of his presence and his sympathy, Mr. Wiley was at last able to hail the day when a very slight improvement manifested itself in the mental condition of his patient, who improved gradually, and surely till he became conscious of the blow which had caused a moral paralysis extending to the period of three months. It is a good sign when a patient requires sympathy and can talk about his sufferings.

Mrs. Stirling, totally unable to comprehend her son, though secretly glad that the engagement had been broken off, affected to display her sympathy by invectives against Miss Singleton, as a heartless girl who had never loved Clement. The superficial woman could not perceive that these reproaches of a woman who was still fondly loved, were agonising to Clement. He had, in the excitement of his feelings, uttered reproaches to Madeline, which, in his sober reflection, he repudiated; and he now confessed to himself that she could not have acted otherwise. Taught by his own sufferings he began to appreciate the agony of Madeline, in immolating her own heart, and preferring duty to love.

Mr. Wiley understood, far better, the human heart. For the present, he uttered no word against Madeline. He sat and listened patiently while Clement raved about her, while he almost maddened himself by dwelling on all the noble qualities, the mental and personal accomplishments of the woman he was never to call his; and waited for the time when all these sufferings could be turned to account. That time was not far distant. In any great and crushing affliction like the death of some dear friend—or what is only less, the death of our hopes from a disappointment similar to that from which Clement was suffering, the human mind in its affliction is peculiarly susceptible of spiritual and religious consolation. There are men who, if you attempted to prove logically that there was a future state of existence, would laugh you to scorn. But let such a one lose a friend —and he believes! The mute eloquence of the grave is more mighty than all theology.

At such a season of affliction, when all the things of the world are "stale, flat, and unprofitable," when life becomes a burthen, and all the ordinary routine of pleasure and profit a loathsome horror, we turn gladly to speculations so utterly foreign to our temporal affairs—as those of a future state.

Wiley took advantage of this phase of Clement's sorrow. The priest placed before the young mourner, books which treated of the happiness of a life devoted to religious meditation and good works, afar from the turmoil, the corroding, cankering cares, the continual disappointments of the giddy, busy world; and when he saw that his pupil's mind was engaged in digesting this food, he artfully and eloquently depicted his (Wiley's) own feelings of thankfulness for the barrier which his religious vows had placed between him and the aimless, senseless, purposeless struggle of men, still vainly persisting in the attempt to find happiness on earth.

It was extremely natural that, in Clement Stirling's depressed condition—the elasticity of hope gone, ordinary pursuits and previous habits of thought rendered distasteful by the rude shock he had received, with no philosophy or experience of life to teach him that such mental clouds would be dispelled, and disclose the sun of a bright, happy future,—it was natural that he should accept and welcome the train of thought which offered an immediate alleviation. Clement fell into the mistake so frequent with young men and women in similar circumstances. Temporarily disgusted with life, he thought himself for ever weaned from the world. He spent long hours, frequently whole days, in ecstatic reveries, which were so much the more agreeable from their contrast to those hours of mental prostration and hypochondria previously experienced. He began to cherish the idea, that were he thoroughly to withdraw from secular pursuits, he would enjoy the moral certainty of his eternal happiness.

To such an extent did he carry this dangerous intoxication of the spirit, that when Wiley, with deliberate abruptness, attempted to engage him on some worldly topic, the words jarred on the enthralled mind of the dreamer, and made earthly cares seem tenfold more impertinent than before. He began seriously to meditate some plan of avoiding the career which his name and station marked out for him, and consulted Wiley on the subject. The young man admired the priest's serene mind, unruffled by the breath of passion, unsullied by the sordid pursuits of worldly ambition, which, to his view—jaundiced by affliction—seemed utterly mischievous.

Clement placed himself mentally in the same situation, and indulged in visions of a life devoted to the service of God. King Henry the Sixth, painted by Shakspeare, not as the imbecile of the chroniclers, but as a noble nature, whose peaceful virtues utterly unqualified him for the age in which he lived, exclaims:

> "O God! methinks it were a happy life
> To be no better than a homely swain."

The unhappy king's soliloquy on the delights of a peaceful life, in the midst of a civil war, is beautifully illustrative of the universal longing of the human mind to escape from a state of anguish to one of repose. Such were the feelings of Clement Stirling, when he pictured to himself the life of a parish priest, as the best refuge from care and trouble.

He consulted Mr. Wiley as to the advisability of taking orders. To the young man's astonishment, his friend opposed the scheme, and even argued against it with a show of warmth. But the arguments which Mr. Wiley used, found no echo in the heart of Clement, probably because they did not come from the heart of the speaker. The priest harped on inducements which he well knew had no weight at that moment with Clement, half broken-hearted and hating life; such, for instance, as the young man's duties to society; of his stake in the county, as the representative of property; of worldly ambition; of a political career; and finally, of falling in love again, and marrying.

But for the gravity of the speaker, and the implicit confidence placed in his sincerity, Clement would have imagined that Mr. Wiley was talking ironically, so utterly misplaced did such representations appear to him in his then condition. He hated society and the world; ambition seemed to him only viler than the pursuit of gold; and as for love—he loathed the very name. Disenchanted of his illusions, and thinking himself wronged because Madeline had not sacrificed all for him, his mind underwent a powerful re-action. His ideal did not exist, therefore love did not exist. The books which he had been reading —monkish legends—the writings of the fathers, and other religious celibates, were not calculated to make him believe in the existence of pure, honourable love—and in his reply to Mr. Wiley he quoted with bitterness the lines which Byron puts into the mouth of Lucifer:

> "But, if that high thought were
> Link'd to a servile mass of matter, and,
> Knowing such things, aspiring to such things,
> And science still beyond them, were chain'd down
> To the most gross and petty paltry wants,
> All foul and fulsome, and the very best
> Of thine enjoyments a sweet degradation,
> A most enervating and filthy cheat
> To lure thee on to the renewal of
> Fresh souls and bodies, all foredoom'd to be
> As frail, and few so happy —— ——"

How utterly unhinged must Clement's mind have been when he could adopt these terrible lines, mocking and caricaturing in a truly devilish spirit the beautiful instinct of nature, and wisely supposed to be the utterance of the arch-enemy of man.

Mr. Wiley only replied with commonplaces, that Clement was young, that his present dislike to the world would not continue. Nettled at this seeming want of sympathy, Clement asked the Priest why he tried to dissuade him from a profession which he had himself embraced.

"Dissuade you from taking orders, my dear Stirling? God forbid that I should do anything of the kind; but it is my duty to tell you that you seem to me not to have sufficiently weighed the grand and stupendous step you speak off. To be a priest, it is not only necessary that an individual should feel a special, natural aptitude for the vocation, but that this bent should be carefully cultivated from his tenderest years. Pardon me for saying that Holy Church does not select for the stewards of her divine mysteries men who, in a fit of misanthropy and disgust with the world, imagine themselves devout because they have been crossed in love. Her servants must be enrolled willingly, not reluctantly. It is not enough that they dislike the world. They must also love religion. They must have experienced a Divine call."

Following up this crafty exordium, Mr. Wiley continued apparently to dissuade Clement Stirling from becoming a priest, while every word tended to confirm the infatuated young man in his resolution. The picture which the ecclesiastic gave of the self-denying life of a Romish pastor, repaid for all worldly sacrifices by the applause of conscience, and the daily, hourly sense of a mind at peace—recommended itself irresistibly to the aspiration of Clement Stirling, who was at the same time, piqued to hear his own convictions spoken of in such a slighting manner as a mere temporary impulse. Assuredly Mr. Wiley understood human nature, and especially the disposition of him on whom he was so skilfully practising.

While in this critical frame of mind, Clement Stirling read in one of the county journals the following paragraph :—

"We have much pleasure in announcing that the health of Miss Singleton, the lovely and accomplished daughter of our member, Colonel Singleton, was sufficiently improved to permit that young lady to be presented at the drawing-room held on Thursday. We congratulate the gallant Colonel that his interesting relative has now taken her place in metropolitan society—a sphere in which she will shine one of the most resplendent luminaries. Also on another piece of intelligence which has come to our ears, viz., that a match is on the *tapis*, and will soon be, if it is not already finally arranged, between Miss Singleton and the Hon. Captain Darton. How true is the remark of the poet :—

'None but the brave deserve the fair.'"

CHAPTER VII.

THE RUBICON IS PASSED.

WHAT trifles decide human destiny! The information conveyed in the elegant specimen of provincial journalism at the close of the last chapter, in addition to some flying rumours which had for some time freely circulated among the country gossips, to the effect that Miss Singleton had made quite a sensation in London, that she went very much into society, and had many admirers, removed the last lingering hope which had rested in Clement's mind that Madeline still loved him, and might at some future period become his. He sought his mother and communicated to her abruptly his intention of taking orders as a Romish priest.

Mrs. Stirling was shocked at this communication. The dearest wish of her heart had been accomplished when her son became a Roman Catholic. Her principal object had been to secure her son's eternal welfare, for she believed, as she had been taught, that there was no certainty of salvation out of the pale of 'The Church,' a doctrine which seems monstrous to every one when arrogated by any other religion than that to which the individual himself belongs. Mrs. Stirling had a secondary and ambitious object. She desired her son to contract a matrimonial alliance with a good family of his own faith, and to enter parliament in the Catholic interest. She had communicated these views to Mr. Wiley, who acted as her temporal as well as spiritual adviser, and he had, as far as words went, given them his entire approval. Too late Mrs. Stirling began to suspect that the man in whom she had placed such implicit confidence had played a double part. She grew jealous of Mr. Wiley's influence over her son, but before breaking with him, she tried the effect of prayers and entreaties in combatting Clement's resolution.

The miserable mother, who saw her son about to be thus taken from her, to become as it were virtually dead to her, detailed to Clement all her worldly plans for advancing his interest. But a fatal barrier to perfect sympathy had been erected between the mother and the son. She was now reaping the harvest of her own sowing. *Her* views seemed to Clement, at that crisis, eminently sordid and prosaic. *His* appeared to her quixotic and unnatural. To his asseverations, made with all the ardour and emphasis of youthful zeal, that he desired to take holy orders from principle; from a sincere conviction that thus he should best work out the salvation of his soul, by assisting to save the souls of others; that worldly ambition was dead within his heart; that the busy world and the ordinary pursuits of men were hateful to him; that he coveted nothing beyond the humble but useful sphere of a parish priest; his mother continually repeated the stereotyped phrases that he was young, without experience; that he had the world before him; and that it would be shameful to throw away his ample advantages of birth, fortune, and abilities. These arguments made no impression on Clement. He did not then know that age and experience gave a value to counsel apparently most common-place. His mother could not enter into his spiritual ambition. How then could he sympathise with her sublunary views?

Mrs. Stirling then lost her temper and played her last card. She accused Mr. Wiley of having used his power to undermine her maternal influence; of having persuaded her son to this step. Clement was irritated at a charge which seemed to him so unjust. He warmly defended Mr. Wiley, and informed his mother that the priest had actually dissuaded him from taking orders. Finally an appeal was made to Mr. Wiley in person. The Jesuit was quite equal to the difficult part he had to play. He professed to side with Mrs. Stirling, and used some commonplace arguments which, as before, served in reality to confirm Clement's resolution. Mrs. Stirling saw too late that she was betrayed. Indignantly she taxed the priest with ingratitude, with repaying her favour and protection by robbing her of her only son, and accused him of cherishing the most interested designs under the mask of holiness. She would listen to no reply, no justification on Mr. Wiley's part, but declared her intention, if Clement did not forthwith relinquish all ideas of becoming a priest, of separating from her son for ever. Under these circumstances Mr. Wiley, finding Clement peremptory, at length, professed to be convinced, and declared his solemn conviction that the young man had a vocation for the priesthood, and that he saw the finger of Providence in all the afflictions which had led to his adoption of the sacred profession.

In due time, Clement Stirling, having undergone the necessary examinations, (his time of probation being merely nominal, owing to the sponsorship of Mr. Wiley) was ordained a deacon of the Catholic Church, and a year afterwards, a priest.

Had it been his lot to have remained in the country parish—where he officiated for four years and upwards—he might have lived a useful and honourable life; happy in his illusions, seeing only the bright side of the religion he had embraced, he might have gone respected and contented to his grave. But this was not to be; the conversion of a gentleman of independent property made a noise in the county, and when Clement Stirling became a priest, his choice excited general comment, and made him a celebrity. He was warmly welcomed by the Catholic gentry of the neighbourhood, and persons of all denominations betrayed a lively interest in the man who could forfeit such excellent worldly prospects for the lowly career of a provincial pastor.

Independently of these incidental causes of interest, Father Stirling made himself remarkable by his personal conduct. He discharged with indefatigable zeal and ardour all the duties of his profession; he was never weary of visiting the poor; he used the ample means at his disposal to relieve their necessities; he preached the gospel with a simple earnestness, which gained many proselytes, and he taught, not merely by precept, but by the whole example of his life. Even the Protestant rector had no fault to find with him, but that he was a papist. Thus the conversion or perversion, as it was styled by adherents of the two creeds, of Clement Stirling to Popery, which might have been only a nine-days' wonder, became a subject of continued interest in the provincial community, and for many miles round. Even those who see an unworthy personal motive in every step of which they do not approve, found it difficult to show what worldly advantage a man of property and position could gain by becoming a Catholic priest in a protestant country. However, it was agreed that there *was* an interested motive somewhere. It actuated Wiley, if not Stirling, who, if not an accomplice, was a victim. The priest wished to secure Stirling's fortune—but then the latter did not go into a monastery—did not surrender his fortune, but used it to good purpose. No matter; the prophets of evil said, time would show that Wiley had interested motives; was he not a Jesuit, &c.?

There is one advantage in being attacked—that one generally meets with some defenders—if not from charity or friendship—from difference of opinion and love of contradiction. This gossip, for and against, made father Stirling a provincial celebrity. His Christian conduct mitigated the scandal caused by his apostacy from the Church of England. It began to be admitted that whatever were his theological errors, he was a good man. When he preached, the chapel was always crowded; for he did not—like most young ecclesiastics of all churches—try to show off his theological learning. His sermons were not of that kind which please some, at the expense of others; they were more moral than doctrinal. He did not "deal damnation round the land" on all he judged his foes, and his friends prophesied that he would rise in the church.

Clement Stirling had been four years engaged in his ministry, when it was intimated to him that his good conduct and abilities had attracted the attention of his metropolitan, and that it was not thought advisable that his talents should be buried in the obscurity of a country parish. A wider sphere awaited father Stirling. Having sufficiently answered the purpose of his ecclesiastical superiors by edifying the country, he was now to grace the metropolis as a distinguished proselyte who had been rescued from the errors of heresy. For the Catholics parade a converted Protestant, just as the Protestants parade a converted papist. Clement Stirling did not desire this change; ambition had not yet re-awakened in his heart; he loved his provincial cure, where he had made friends, and did not desire to leave it. He had, however, no option. He obeyed the orders of the establishment of which he constituted a mere unit.

In London, Stirling rejoined Wiley, who had returned to the metropolis after his friend had taken orders. One thing tended to reconcile father Stirling to this change in the scene of his duties. It was the reflection that he might be even more useful to his fellow-creatures in London than in the country. His heart ached at the misery he saw around him as he walked with Wiley through the streets of the modern Babylon. He felt ashamed that he had permitted his own personal troubles so totally to absorb him.

At first he stood aghast at the immense amount of the misery with which he desired to grapple; but, recovering from this stupor, he experienced a sensation of thankfulness that his private fortune would enable him to do so much. He consulted with Wiley, frankly communicating his views, anticipating the foundation of ragged schools, and nightly refuges for destitute wretches whose very presence in the streets seemed a libel on the national claim to Christianity. He asked eagerly for introductions to other gentlemen with whom he could co-operate in the good work. In short, he burned with zeal to commence his labours as a home missionary, to preach the gospel to the heathen of London.

Amiable enthusiast! to suppose that a nation so busy in converting the Jews, and sending missionaries to Africa and the Cannibal Islands could be expected to unite to make provision for the physical and spiritual appetites of our starving fellow-countrymen;

or that men will forget theological intolerance in Christian charity!

Wiley, who knew the world, smiled at the eagerness and romantic zeal of the young priest.

"My dear Stirling," he replied, "London is indeed to be the scene of your missionary labours, but these are not exactly the sort of people you are called upon to convert."

"What do you mean?" asked Mr. Stirling, with unaffected surprise.

"Why," said Wiley, "we have plenty of subordinates for that kind of duty; we have scripture readers, and good laymen and women who distribute both spiritual and practical food to these poor people."

"Have you?" interrupted the young man. "Then, why are they so miserable, so destitute? I meet unfortunates who are literally nearly naked, and their bones almost starting through their skin; and in walking the streets my ears are assailed by blasphemy which causes me to shudder; these people appear to me to want everything—food, clothes, and religion."

"Well," said Wiley, "we do what we can. You do not understand the world yet. The Protestants hinder us at every step; they will not try to save these persons' souls, nor allow us to save them; they act like the dog in the manger; no sooner does our religion make an effort to extend the gospel into those wretched lanes and back settlements, where the Anglican missionaries care not to penetrate, than Protestant prejudices are stirred against us by the old watch-word of 'No Popery.' But, to permit *you*, with your great talents and sound scholarship, to minister in the slums and alleys of London, would be like setting a high-mettled racer to do the work of a dray-horse. What we are most in want of in England are priests who are gentlemen, to labour as missionaries among the higher classes."

"But the poor," exclaimed Clement, "the starving wretches of Saffron Hill, and those who nightly congregate under the dry arches of the Adelphi—oh, you see I have already made myself acquainted with the haunts of misery in this vast metropolis—the thousands of fallen women who infest the streets—may I not at least be permitted the privilege of relieving cold and hunger, out of my private fortune?"

"My good Stirling," rejoined Wiley, "listen to me, not as your ecclesiastical senior, not as a priest, but as your friend, and one who has been instrumental in causing your removal to London. Your zeal is admirable, and I should be sorry to check it, for, believe me, there is an ample field provided for its display. It has already produced the most favourable results to our cause—I mean the cause of Holy Church in this heretical and backsliding nation. But you must remember that your vocation is to save souls; you cannot take upon yourself the duties of a poor-law commissioner, or a reformatory society; your property would go at once, if you gave a loose to your generous impulses, and it would be consumed without the least appreciable benefit; in the ocean of London pauperism, it would be like a drop in the bucket; besides, we cannot undertake indiscriminate relief. Charity begins at home; we must attend to our own poor, before we save protestants. But do not be uneasy; there will be a noble field for all your enthusiasm and benevolence, and rest assured that among the upper, and the wealthy middle classes, there is as much, if not more need of religion, than among the poor."

I have now brought the story down to the period at which the scene described in the first Chapter occurred, and have, I hope, enabled the reader to form some conception of the character of Father Stirling; but that character was to be still more developed by trials far more afflicting than those through which he had already passed.

BOOK II.

CHAPTER I.

A DEVOTED PARISH PRIEST.

For two years Father Stirling pursued his avocations of a priest in London, too much absorbed by the strange volume of experience opened to him by his profession to turn his eyes inwards; to ask himself if he were as happy as he might be, whether he had chosen his career well or wisely. No better proof of his sincerity and singleness of heart could be desired than the fact that he had not been spoiled by his great success as a pulpit orator. Regarding himself merely in the light of a humble minister of Providence, he was not dazzled or rendered vain-glorious by the fame he had so suddenly achieved. For he might have said of himself, as Byron did, that he woke up and found himself famous. And of all kinds of fame, that of an eloquent clergyman is the most trying to its possessor. To be fêted, cajoled, caressed, flattered, and idolized, especially by female parishioners, as a saint, as a man of God, frequently has the effect of causing the idol to display to the keen and scrutinizing observer, the feet of clay.

It was not so with Father Stirling, though of course there were malicious persons to say that he was like other men, that he was a *Tartufe*, a Jesuit in disguise, &c. Yet it was extremely difficult—it might be said, impossible—for any one to nurse these prejudices after looking upon the man's face, or hearing him preach. Truth, manhood, and sincerity, generally reveal themselves in the most unmistakeable manner in the countenance and voice. This man, after preaching to a crowded congregation, holding sinners breathless with his words, would descend from the pulpit, divest himself of his sacredotal costume, and slip away from the chancel door, in order to avoid the multitude of curious spectators who lingered to see him come out. He never permitted himself the luxury of a cab, unless when pressed for time. Lost among the pedestrians of London, the man so lately the cynosure of all regards, would trudge home to his humble apartments in Gloucester Street, Queen's Square. The house belonged to him; he had bought it, indeed, from a grasping and avaricious landlord, that he might permit a decayed family, who were about to be turned into the streets, to live in it rent-free; yet these recipients of his bounty never knew who their benefactor was. The priest—whom they imagined to be poor—represented himself merely as the agent of a benevolent Catholic lady.

Father Stirling occupied the upper part of the house; his housekeeper had been a poor old apple-woman, one of those unfortunate beings whom we see sitting shivering in the streets over their little stock of merchandise, preferring to perish slowly of cold and hunger, rather than curtail their liberty by going into the workhouse ; perhaps, too, there is a small modicum of dignity and self-respect left in their poor, withered bosoms. Why not! they are still human, what is left of them. What a problem for solution, what a subject of meditation do these poor people present to the large-hearted, and large-minded spectator! What a sermon does their mute, uncomplaining sufferings preach to the rich as they roll by in their carriages!

This poor woman, Hannah McKay, was not a Catholic, and father Stirling had made no attempt to convert her; he did not think it right to attempt to unsettle her religious belief in the evening of her days; and when this good man alleviated distress, he did not stop to enquire what was the creed of the sufferer, unless, of course, he was asked for spiritual consolation. The poor woman, thus furnished with a comfortable home, and enabled to do something for a daughter who was in service, regarded father Stirling more as a saint than a man. She was never weary of repeating his praises when she had the opportunity, and thought she never could sufficiently evince her gratitude for what he had done for herself, little imagining that the priest had been already repaid by the applause of conscience, and the daily sight of one whom he had rescued from suffering and misery.

Hannah's only cause of complaint against her master was that he would not take sufficient care of himself, or allow her to make him sufficiently comfortable. The rooms occupied by father Stirling were certainly those of an anchorite; common chintz curtains covered the windows; the floor was uncarpeted, save by a small piece in the centre, and a mat, which Hannah had insisted upon putting down, contrary to express orders; an ordinary deal table, and a few windsor chairs, with an old arm-chair, formed the furniture. The only things in the shape of ornament were a tolerably-large and well-filled book-case of painted wood, a beautiful painting of the Virgin, and a crucifix. In every other respect the walls, covered with a cheap paper, representing a pattern of white leaves and flowers on a drab ground, were perfectly bare, displaying a monotony offensive to the spectator's eyes.

Father Stirling never took food more than twice a-day, and then very sparingly. Frequently when Hannah had taken particular pains to prepare some dish which she hoped would tempt his appetite, she would find, to her great mortification, that it had been left untasted; when she came up to remove the breakfast or supper tray, she would find the priest absorbed in his breviary, or some other work, and Hannah's *chef d'œuvre* in cookery quite cold and untouched. On such occasions the poor woman could not always control her vexation, and when father Stirling perceived this, he frequently ate a little on purpose that she might not suppose he slighted her skill in the culinary art.

If it is creditable to the poor to support their enforced poverty with resignation, how much more creditable is it to those who, having wealth, actuated by the purest motives, prefer to live as if they were poor. There was no affectation in father Stirling's meagre manner of living; he acted from strictly conscientious motives, believing that as a Christian minister, he had no moral right to spend on himself more than was absolutely sufficient to obtain the necessaries of life. He used frequently to charge himself with luxury, when he compared his own condition with that of the poor whom he met in the streets.

Independently moreover of these religious motives to poverty, his tastes prompted him to a sublime indifference to that vulgar luxury which is characteristic of ordinary and common-place minds. Many superior men entertain this contempt for good living, for costly furniture, and all those unnecessary and superfluous artificial social appliances, deprived of which, multitudes of men and women would be utterly miserable. This is not, however, a characteristic of *all* superior minds. Many intellectual people are as greedy of comfort and luxury as the most ignorant and unrefined, who place their social status in money and money's worth, and pride themselves on having everything comfortable about them.

Father Stirling was remarkable even among his brethren for the intrepid discharge of his clerical duties. In his visitations, the only difference he made between the rich and the poor, was to stay longer in the dwellings of the latter than in those of the former. He entered fearlessly into the hovels of the sick poor. No form of contagious disease, no amount of squalid misery deterred him. And all that central portion of London, known as St. Giles', was far worse than it is now. To be sure the Roman Catholic Clergy are distinguished for their contempt of death in the discharge of duty; but Father Stirling was noted as being the bravest among the brave, and laid himself open to serious expostulation from friends, and even rebuke from his ecclesiastical superiors, for so freely exposing his valuable life. But youth is the season of bravery; and youth, fortified by religious zeal, is reckless of danger. Father Stirling persisted in bending over the dying, to catch the last whispered confession, and to utter in the ear of the departing the talismanic words which enable the sinner to die in peace, and to exclaim triumphantly in the very moment of dissolution,

"O death, where is thy sting? O grave, where is thy victory?"

The impunity with which he visited patients ill of small pox, fever, and other contagious diseases, encouraged among the poorer and more ignorant portion of the Catholic community, the idea that this man was especially favoured by Divine Providence. No belief appears more natural to persons unacquainted with the general laws which govern the universe. To people who thus confound the moral and physical world, it appears a strange inexplicable thing that a good man should meet his fate while alleviating the sufferings of his fellow-men.*

Such then was the life led by this good parish priest, spending his youth, his energy, his fortune—everything in the service of his

* "With regard to the innocence of the suffering parties, there is one important consideration which is pressed upon us from many quarters—namely, that moral conditions have not the least concern in the working of the physical laws. These arrangements proceed with an entire independence of all such conditions, and desirably so, for otherwise there would be no certain dependence placed upon them. Thus it may happen that of two persons ascending a piece of scaffolding, the one a virtuous, the other a vicious man, the former, being the less cautious of the two, ventures upon an insecure place, falls, and is killed, while the other, choosing a better footing, remains uninjured. It is not in what we can conceive of the nature of things, that there should be a special exemption from the ordinary laws of matter, to save this virtuous man. So it might be, that of two physicians attending fever cases in a mean part of a large city, the one, an excellent citizen, may stand in such a position with respect to the beds of the patients, as to catch the infection, of which he dies in a few days, while the other, a bad husband and father, and who, unlike the former, only attends such cases with selfish ends, takes care to be as much as possible out of the stream of infection, and accordingly escapes. In both these cases man's sense of good and evil—his faculty of conscientiousness—would incline him to destine the vicious man to destruction, and save the virtuous. But the Great Ruler of Nature does not act on such principles. He has established laws for the operation of inanimate matter, which are quite unswerving, so that when we know them, we have only to act in a certain way with respect to them, in order to obtain all the benefits and avoid all the evils connected with them."—*Vestiges of the Natural History of Creation.*

fellow-men. If self-sacrifice can make a human being happy, then father Stirling ought to have been happy, or at least contented. Yet he was not. He was respected, loved, almost venerated by his poor parishioners. He was doing his duty conscientiously. He performed works of supererogation. He entertained the belief that he was in the right way; in submitting himself implicitly to the delegated authority residing in the Church, he held the hope that he was working out his salvation; what more then, was required to render the good man happy? Such was the constitution of father Stirling's mind that exactly in proportion as he regulated his own life; as he weaned himself from selfish and worldly lusts, did he suffer from reflecting on the miserable condition of mankind! We have seen that this priest was not bigoted. It was not merely their spiritual state, the absence of belief, their moral and religious destitution; it was the actual physical sufferings he saw on every side which distressed him.

He, a man tenderly nurtured, with every want supplied, his mind and heart rendered eminently susceptible by all his previous education, had been thrown suddenly into a calling which brought him into immediate daily contact with sin, vice, misery and want. Often would he leave his house in a tolerably equable state of mind, and before he had got fifty yards, his heart would be torn with the spectacle of some horrible suffering which he was powerless to alleviate. At such moments it seemed strange to this sincere Christian that the sun should shine, that the birds should sing, that nature should show no sympathy, and that men and women should pass on their way to profit and pleasure so careless and indifferent. Then he would propound puzzling questions to himself, in which his faith and his experience seemed totally at variance. In the paroxysms of these mental conflicts his conscience would cry,—"What, why and wherefore is this strange problem of human misery? Why do not good, believing, charitable men join together to banish suffering, or at least to reduce it to an inappreciable minimum?"

As Father Stirling was forced to frequent the houses of the luxurious and opulent, these impressions were continually heightened by the effect of contrast. He passed from the atmosphere of respectability and virtue, surrounded by splendour sustained by wealth, (where the ready supply of every physical and intellectual want, the result of an elaborate social structure, erected an artificial barrier against temptation, which was complacently attributed by the persons so favoured to the protection of a special Providence,) to dens of vice, poverty, and crime, where wretches alternately denied the existence of, and railed against a God, who permitted them to starve. On one of these occasions, when the priest was endeavouring to awaken a dying infidel to some sense of a hereafter, the answer he received was in these words:—"Why does not God do something for us here? A pretty

God to let his creatures starve." And with this blasphemy on his lips, the man died. But all unbelievers were not of this kind. On another occasion the words of a dying man were as follows:—"I am going to discover the great secret. I respect you, sir, as a man, not as a priest. I have always considered all religions as human impositions, and I am not going to die with a lie on my lips. I believe death to be an eternal sleep, but whether I am right or wrong I wish no priestly mummery to take place over my remains."

Father Stirling's painful experience taught him that what is called death-bed repentance, is generally a fallacy. That it is in reality the result of fear, and that it is contrary to all our conceptions of Divine justice or mercy to represent God as determining the eternal destiny of a human being, by his conduct in his last moments. The real penitent does not wait for the approach of death to repent of his sins. A practical proof of the error of attributing this undue importance to the last moments o life, is the fact that the wicked have died calmly, and the good have often showed the greatest terror of death. The dread of dissolution would appear to be with the majority, a constitutional fear which no faith or hope of eternity can remove. Dr. Johnson, eminent for orthodoxy, had an uncontrollable terror of death.

CHAPTER II.

FROM THE BALL-ROOM TO THE CONDEMNED CELL.

On one occasion Father Stirling had been induced to break through his strict routine of living, so far as to be present at a large evening assembly given by Lady Oldtowers, whose husband was the representative of an old Catholic family. The priest's scruples had been vanquished by the representations of the hostess that there could be nothing contrary to ecclesiastical etiquette in being present, as other Catholic clergymen attended. She added, moreover, that the presence of these holy men always made her conscience easier while enjoying the legitimate pleasures of the world.

Father Stirling allowed himself to be persuaded, and went to this ball; but, as usual, he left strict orders with his house-keeper that whatever message came for him in his absence should be forwarded to him at Lady Oldtowers' residence in Berkeley Square. At ten o'clock a message was accordingly forwarded to Father Stirling of a singular and exceptional nature. A felon, convicted of murder, and lying in the condemned cell at Newgate, desired to confess to Father Stirling. This information was conveyed in a note written by the governor of the gaol, and forwarded by an express messenger. Father Stirling happened to be standing by the lady of the house when the note was brought to him by a servant. Making an apology, he opened the note and read it. He turned very pale, and betrayed other signs of agitation.

"What is the matter, your Reverence? No bad news, I hope," said Lady Oldtowers.

Mr. Stirling replied by placing the note in her hands, being at the moment too much agitated to speak. Lady Oldtowers read the note with eyes sparkling with indignation.

"This is infamous!" she exclaimed. "This must be intended as a purely gratuitous insult."

Father Stirling looked at her with astonishment and curiosity. Lady Oldtowers continued:

"I shall speak to my husband. He must bring this matter before Parliament."

"Pray what does your ladyship mean?" said the priest.

"Do you not consider it an indignity, an insult that the governor of Newgate should write to you to discharge this loathsome duty? Would not any ordinary priest do as well? This is evidently a Protestant insult aimed at our holy religion in the person of one of its most eminent professors. And to send at this hour in the evening—"

"Yes," interrupted the priest. "The affair must, indeed, be urgent. I must go at once."

"Your Reverence need not leave us. You

will find writing materials in the library. You can refer him to another priest, and I trust at the same time your charity will not hinder you from expressing your surprise that *you* should have been selected—"

"Excuse me, your ladyship; the messenger is waiting. I will accompany him to Newgate. There is perhaps not a moment to be lost."

Lady Oldtowers looked aghast.

"You cannot possibly mean that you intend to go. Pray consider, my dear Mr. Stirling, a murderer—the condemned cell in Newgate! How frightful! and then the actual risk to your valuable life. There is always malignant fever in these gaols."

With a rapid adieu, Father Stirling hastened away. He had heard Lady Oldtowers' last words, and remembered them afterwards, although too much preoccupied at the moment to appreciate all their heartless selfishness.

Never to his dying day, and in spite of the most heart-rending personal sorrows, did

Father Stirling forget his experience of that memorable evening. Surely it was impossible for the force of contrast to go further. To leave a scene of life, light, splendour, festivity, gaiety, luxury, where ladies and gentlemen were killing the time with fashionable folly, "pricking it to death with pins," to be alone with a murderer in the condemned cell at Newgate! My pen trembles, my heart sickens at the horrible scene I am about to describe; but it is necessary to the truth of this history, to display this evidence of Father Stirling's moral courage; and moreover this episode has its lesson.

The good and brave priest, who had faced all kinds of horrors with comparative stoicism, trembled as he got out of the vehicle which had drawn up in the deep shadow of the blackened walls of Newgate prison, and heard the unbarring and unlocking of the outer door.

"Sir," said the attendant turnkey, "would you like to see the governor first?"

"No," said Mr. Stirling, "let me first see the unhappy man."

"Beg pardon, sir," added the man; "but you're evidently not used to this sort of thing. Better have a sip of this; it will steady your nerves—keep you from turning faint-like," and he held out a small flask which he took from his pocket, which the priest declined.

"No offence, I hope, sir. This way, sir."

On their way through a flagged court-yard the turnkey touched his hat respectfully to a tall, imposing-looking man, who proved to be the governor of the prison. He addressed Father Stirling, and apologized for having written to him, stating that he should not have taken such a liberty but for the request of the convict, who had particularly mentioned his (Father Stirling's) name, and when asked if any Catholic priest would not serve, replied that he would see no one else.

"Under these circumstances," added the governor, "I thought it my duty to accede to this unfortunate man's request—the last wishes of a dying man—for unless a reprieve comes, which I do not expect, Hoskins will die the day after to-morrow."

Father Stirling shuddered as he replied:

"You have done right; I thank you, sir."

The turnkey paced on before; Father Stirling followed, his eyes fixed on the ground; his fingers mechanically telling the beads of a rosary which he carried in his pocket, too much absorbed in anticipation of the work before him to be conscious of the scenes through which he was passing.

They passed over some flag-stones, which showed signs of having been recently raised. It was the spot under which had been buried, with plenty of quicklime, the corpse of the last criminal hanged in front of Newgate. Fortunately for Father Stirling he passed this spot unconsciously. They entered that part of the prison appropriated to the condemned cells. The turnkey stopped abruptly before a strong oaken door, deeply imbedded in the massive stone wall, applied the key to the wards of the lock, and threw the door open. This process occupied about half a minute, and during that interval the feelings of Father Stirling were wrought up to such a pitch of excitement that it was a positive relief to him, when reality supeseded to anticipation, and he stood within the condemned cell.

"Do you wish to be left alone with him, sir?" said the turnkey, in an under tone.

"Of course," replied the priest.

"Very good, sir," said the man, who added as he glanced at Father Stirling's emaciated and stooping figure, "Let me advise you, sir, not to go within reach of him. He's very violent sometimes, and I don't think he's quite right in his head."

After giving this caution to the priest whose "pluck" he greatly admired, the man left the cell. Father Stirling at first believed himself alone, for in the dim light of that dismal place he could at first distinguish no one. No sooner, however, had the turnkey's footsteps ceased to sound on the stone pavement, without, than from a deep shadow in the farthest corner of the dungeon a man started erect upon his feet. The movement was so abrupt and unexpected that the priest involuntarily stepped back towards the door, under the impression that he was about to be attacked, and then stood gazing at the horrible aspect presented by the figure, who stood clanking his chains before him. The light which came through a "bull's-eye" grating set in the door, made the prisoner dimly visible from out a mass of shadow, like a picture by Rembrandt. Father Stirling never could forget the expression of that face, the matted hair, the pallid haggard features, the bloodshot eyes, the clasped and manacled hands, and the sound of that voice.

CHAPTER III.

CAPITAL PUNISHMENT.

"WHAT," cried the condemned, "do *you* fear me? O, my God, do you think I would harm *you*, my deliverer, my saviour. Quick, quick, are you listening to me? There is no time to be lost."

"There is, indeed, no time to be lost," said the priest, recovering himself. "Kneel with me, my brother, and let us pray together. It will compose your mind for confession."

"It is not that—it is not that," cried the man, with a horrible eagerness. "I have no confession to make. I am not guilty, you know, I pleaded 'not guilty,' and if they hang me it will be legal murder. It was a case of justifiable manslaughter; but listen, do you know why I have sent for you," he plucked from his breast a newspaper, and pointed to a paragraph highly laudatory of Father Stirling. "Ever since I read this, some weeks ago, I have said this man is not an ordinary priest; he is a saint. He goes about doing good. He is rich, yet he is humble, and spends his wealth on the poor, and he has great influence. The rich, the powerful, flock to hear him preach. This man has the power to save me if he will."

"I have the will, but I have no power," said the priest.

"Yes, yes," continued the man, with frenzied eagerness. "You have the power. You are universally respected; you are a holy man; you are one of God's ministers, and you are 'eloquent.' So the paper says. You can talk to any one. There are none so great or powerful, but you can talk to. Aha! do you understand now? You will go, will you not, at once to the judge, or to the great personage, who orders me to be executed, and say that it is a mistake, that I am not guilty of deliberate murder, and that the verdict should have been, as my lawyer said it would be, justifiable homicide; and if they are obstinate, you must plead for me; you must melt them with pity, and if they still remain obstinate, if they say I am condemned by the law, and must suffer, you must at least demand a reprieve. Oh, they cannot, they will not, they dare not refuse that. You will soothe and threaten by turns. You will denounce God's anger against them, you will excommunicate them, if they refuse it. You will say that even if I were guilty, which I am not, that I have not repented, have not confessed, and that I am not fit to die in my present condition, and then—do you hear—if they grant me a reprieve I swear before God I will repent and confess, and prepare for death. But now I cannot, it is too sudden. I must have time. The chaplain has been here tormenting me, and accusing me of hardness of heart, because I will not, because I cannot listen to him. It is not so. I am not hardened. I tried to pray, and could not. My thoughts wandered. He does not understand, you see. It is his duty, and he talks to me just as he talks to others. He does not know, nor the judge who put on the black cap to sentence me, does not know, what the fear of death is. When he talks of the mercy of God, I only see before me the scaffold. I saw a man hung once when I was a boy, and I have never forgotten it; but, no—they will not—they cannot hang me, for I am unfit to die. I have led a wicked life. I have blasphemed and offended God, and He will not listen to me. How can I repent if God has hardened my heart. No, no—a reprieve—a reprieve—a reprieve!"

He yelled out the last words, and fell down foaming at the mouth. The priest's blood ran cold in his veins, as he looked upon that writhing mass of clothes and irons, and thought that *there* was a human soul condemned by his fellow men, to stand in a few hours before the judgment seat of God, and receive his sentence of eternal weal or woe. He tried in vain to recall the convict to a state of resignation; the unhappy man only kept repeating that he was totally unfit to meet death, and that he would not confess unless he had more time. In that moment the priest's resolution was taken. He saw that the man was unfit to meet death in his present condition, and determined to try at least to procure him a reprieve. At this instant the turnkey entered hurriedly.

When they were without the cell, he said to the priest:

"I told you he was very violent, sir."

Before quitting the gaol, Father Stirling had a brief interview with the governor, who expressed a hope that the prisoner had benefited by his exhortations. On hearing the priest's reply, the governor shook his head, and said he had feared it, and that the convict would not listen to the chaplain, &c. When Father Stirling communicated his intention of seeking an interview with the Home Secretary, the governor assured him that it would be useless. This, however, did not in the least shake the priest's determination. He had always entertained the strongest objection to capital punishment, and now that the question had come before him from a point of view so frightfully practical, he felt compelled by conscience to protest on behalf of this criminal and others.

He succeeded, though with much difficulty, in obtaining an audience of the Home Secretary, who heard his arguments with courtesy, and then replied:

"Reverend sir, though I respect your zeal as a minister of Christ, I can hold out no hopes to this wretched man. He has been tried and convicted on the clearest evidence of a deliberate murder. Society must protect itself. The law must take its course."

"But, sir," persevered Father Stirling, "granted that this man's life is justly forfeited to the law of the land, our merciful religion says that, however great the crime, repentance will insure the pardon of God. The judge who condemned this man hoped that God would have mercy on his guilty soul. He has been allowed just two weeks to repent. The time is too short. The man still persists in denying his guilt. His fear of death is so great that he is incapable of listening to spiritual exhortation. Under these circumstances, you will surely grant a reprieve. Give me time to bring him to a more befitting frame of mind. Do not send him to meet the Almighty Judge with a lie in his mouth. This is to destroy the soul as well as the body. I am one of that rapidly increasing number who think that we have no right to take away human life; that the mysterious principle which God gives, God alone should extinguish. But, at any rate, do not doom this man's soul to everlasting perdition. Allow me to return and comfort this unhappy man with the tidings of a respite, and I do not doubt that, by the blessing of God I shall bring him to confess his crime and recognise the justice of his punishment—in short, to meet his doom as he ought. Oh, sir, think on the inconsistency between faith and practice; between the Christianity which we profess, and the laws which we put in force. In the same breath that we tell the sinner that he may expect pardon from God, we, his fellow-men, show ourselves relentless; this is virtually to say that the sinner too vile for earth is fit for Heaven. How can we pretend that capital punishment is founded on God's law. How can we say to our erring brother, God will pardon you *there*, but commands us not to pardon you *here*."

"Mr. Stirling," said the Home Secretary, "you must excuse me, but all this is quite irrelevant. I regret as deeply as yourself the impenitent state of this man; but the agony suffered by one criminal is not to weigh for an instant against the safety of millions. Society must protect itself, and a man who can commit a murder in cold blood deserves no pity."

"The law of capital punishment," replied the priest, "is based upon revenge, a principle which Christianity repudiates."

"If it be so," returned the Home Secretary quickly, "why do the ministers of Christianity announce an eternity of punishment for sinners? Human vengeance is at least accountable on the plea of safety to the many by putting the wicked to death, and also as a salutary warning to sinners; but I have always been at a loss to comprehend what moral purpose could be subserved by an eternity of Divine vengeance. But my time is too precious, Mr. Stirling, to discuss either capital punishment or theology. You are young, sir, and may think me cold; but I can assure you it would be a cruelty to this man to grant a reprieve. It would only awaken hopes of pardon, and he would be even less fit to die than he is at present."

Thus the audience terminated.

Philip Hoskins, the convict lying under sentence of death, was an illustration of the old old story in crime. He had never known the care of either father or mother. Turned loose on the world, he had grown up as thousands are growing up, at war with society. Driven into crime by necessity, he had been transported. Under the tyranny of the prison-governor in Norfolk Island, all his bad passions had been fostered. On one occasion while drawn up with his fellow-prisoners for inspection, the convict next to him had spat out a piece of tobacco, the use of which is strictly prohibited. The overseer charged Hoskins with the breach of discipline, who denied it. "Who did it then?" Hoskins replied that he did not know. These unfortunate men are true to one another, proving that if they were treated like men, and not like wild beasts, they might be reclaimed. Hoskins was condemned to receive one hundred lashes. As he was being tied up, he said to the flagellator, "We shall meet again!"

Every man who administers the lash is a marked man among the convicts, and is generally shot by the one whom he has flogged, or by some of his comrades at the first opportunity. On the expiration of his penal term Hoskins returned to England, and succeeded in getting employment at a factory in a provincial town in the west. One day he was abruptly discharged. No other reason was assigned than that he had once been a convict at Norfolk Island. Hoskins succeeded in learning from a fellow-workman the name of the informant. Judge of his feelings when it proved to be that of the man against whom he had already vowed vengeance. He watched his opportunity, recognised his old enemy, the flagellator, and shot him dead as he stood in front of his own door.

Such is a very brief outline of the history of Philip Hoskins, whom Father Stirling in vain tried to save. At the time appointed, this unfortunate man met his doom, and was strangled in front of Newgate. He died impenitent. Father Stirling remained with him to the last moment, in the hope that he might render the convict more fit for death; but in vain. His last hours were spent either in hideous blasphemy, in supplications for a reprieve, or in stolid silence. While he retained the use of his reason he persisted in affirming his innocence, but as the fatal moment approached, his apprehensions produced a perfect stupor of fear. He was obliged to be half carried, half dragged to the scaffold. To crown the effect of this awful tragedy, the sufferer's agony was protracted by some mismanagement on the part of the executioner. Amid the crowd, where blasphemy, ribaldry, and pocket-picking went on as usual, there were about three women to two men. And such scenes are periodically represented in a Christian land! It was the first and last execution ever witnessed by Father Stirling, who did not recover the usual tone of his spirits for many days afterwards.

CHAPTER IV.

ROMAN CATHOLIC DOCTRINES.

In order that the characters of my narrative may present a more life-like appearance, I take the opportunity to refer briefly to the ecclesiastical state of affairs at this period, the commencement of the year 1840. The passing of the Reform Bill in 1832, was a great and bloodless revolution. It had been preceded by Catholic Emancipation in 1829, and was followed in 1833 by the act which gave freedom to eight hundred thousand negroes in the West Indies. In these ecclesiastical and political reforms and the proposed bill for the relief of the Jews, moderate and sensible men saw only simple acts of justice consistent with the growing enlightenment of the times. When the Duke of Wellington declared that while he remained in office, there should be no reform, he spoke with the characteristic bluntness of a soldier who believed that in politics as in military affairs, men must be taught the lesson of prompt obedience to authority. The mob, acting in a spirit of rude justice, broke the windows of the man they had delighted to honour, and to whom so much incense had been, and was subsequently, burnt. A French man writing of England said: "Another statue of Wellington has just been erected opposite Apsley House, for it is necessary to his peace of mind that he should contemplate himself from his drawing-room, as well as from his dining-room windows."

The Tories said the country was going to the devil, while the radicals hailed the approach of a universal franchise and a republic. Mr. Robert Owen, the eminent socialist, said that though there was not one rational man in the world yet, he did not despair of the future of the human race. Daniel O'Connell was agitating for Repeal, while Cobbett, the great English agitator, after having done his work, had been carried to his grave in 1835. The admirable letters of the Rev. Sidney Smith had greatly assisted to bring about Catholic Emancipation by showing the country that the surest and readiest way to check tumult in Ireland and general disaffection among the Catholic Community, was to admit them to the same rights and privileges enjoyed by their fellow subjects. Of course rabid Protestants and rabid Catholics (though with very different feelings) agreed in predicting the same result of Catholic Emancipation—the destruction of the Protestant by the Catholic Religion.

There were, however, several concurrent circumstances to favour the idea that in this phase of the mighty conflict which had for three centuries agitated Christendom, Protestantism was beginning to recede before Catholicism in England. The State Church was becoming unpopular, owing to the frequent disgraceful collisions in levying tithes between the clergy and their flocks, and which led in 1838 to the passing of the bill for the commutation of tithes into money. In January, 1835, a coroner's jury brought in a verdict of wilful murder against the Rev. Archdeacon Ryder, at whose instance the military were employed to enforce the collection of his tithe. In October, 1836, a fatal tithe conflict took place at Dunkerrin, in the diocese of Killaloe, Ireland, in consequence of the employment of the armed police force to serve subpœnas at the suit of Dean Hawkins, who had been an absentee for the previous five or six years, and had but lately returned to the parish. The people resisted the officers and one of the rioters was shot, while Hogan, an officer of the law, was beaten in a dreadful manner."

Such were the announcements which appeared in the papers. Tithe affrays occurred then with about the same frequency as poaching affrays now. A parson collecting his tithes at the point of the bayonet, or selling-up a poor parishioner, does not offer an edifying spectacle. There were, moreover, plenty of "bloated pluralists" and non-resident clergymen, and the bishops had far larger salaries then than now. The State Church, the most richly endowed church in Christendom, presented the painful contrast of bishops, deans, and other dignitaries, living in luxury and opulence, and curates bringing up families on eighty pounds a year. It was no wonder then, that Church Reform was demanded, and that the ranks of the Dissenters were recruited at the expense of the establishment.

There were other causes for the growing unpopularity. Oxford was becoming the head-quarters of schism. Eminent clergymen went over to Rome. Others did not go over to Rome, but the public thought they would have acted more consistently in going, than in staying. They were Romanizing and doing their best, wilfully or unconsciously, to convert their flocks into semi-papists. Among the most eminent of these innovators was Doctor Formula, of whom I shall again have occasion to speak. Every shade of opinion was represented by almost imperceptible gradations, from the extremest latitudinarianism to the strictest orthodoxy. There were High Church, Broad Church, Low Church, and No Church—every variety of belief between that of the Ranters of the Tabernacle or Little Bethel and "The Scarlet Lady," as they politely termed the Church of Rome.

One of the personages of my story, Father Wiley, saw in the present aspect of ecclesiastical affairs great hope for the Papal Cause in England. He was a member of the Society of Jesuits, and he saw things from a Jesuit point of view. The unity and consistency of my narrative demand here a few explanatory remarks on Catholicism and Jesuitism. To the unthinking zealot, who follows blindly the religion learnt in his youth, all others appear more or less incomprehensible and absurd. Thus, to the narrow-minded and bigoted Protestant, Roman Catholicism is as strange and mysterious as Protestantism is strange and mysterious to the bigoted Catholic. Many of my Protestant readers may have never entered a Catholic Church. They may have never associated with Catholics. If they are puzzled to form a correct idea of a bigoted Catholic, they may easily do so by regarding a bigoted Protestant. There are no lack of these to form a study, and as far as my experience goes, there is no appreciable moral difference between bigots of every religion.

Those who love to study the science of man, and the philosophy of history, are enabled to put aside their own private convictions, and enter into the spirit of religions they do not profess. The following very brief review of the genius of Catholicism is a synopsis of a chapter in Comte's Philosophy of the Sciences,* and forms a fitting preface to remarks on Jesuitism.

Whatever may be our speculative opinions, we cannot deny that the Roman Catholic Religion has played a mighty part in the history of mankind. Catholicism introduced a spiritual power entirely distinct from, and utterly independent of, temporal power. Morality penetrated gradually into policy. Thus, in the midst of the feudal period, among orders founded on birth, fortune, or military deserts, the order of the priesthood formed a large and powerful class, in which intellectual and moral superiority proved the title to ascendancy, and presented a realization of the grand Utopia of the Greek philosophers. Cardinals, and Popes were drawn from the lowest class.

The method of electing Popes was a triumph of political wisdom far superior to the empirical expedient of hereditary right.

* Adapted from the work of Mr. Lewis.

The various monastic institutions were admirably adapted to the middle ages, as constituting the cradles in which Christian conceptions, dogmatical and practical, were elaborated. They assisted in that powerful education of the clergy which was evinced in the superiority of ecclesiastical genius, and which enabled the priests to become the teachers and rulers of mankind.

Whatever we may *now* think of Papal Infallibility, it constituted *then* a great intellectual and social progress; it restrained the right of supernatural inspiration to the supreme Pontiff. The spirit of Protestantism tends directly to augment, not to restrict, the right of Divine inspiration. Catholicism holds that Divine inspiration is immanent in the Church, but she considerately restricts its manifestation to rare instances, refusing to ratify, unless with the most careful scrutiny and solemn deliberation, the claim of an individual to this distinction. Some Protestant sects adopt the reverse principle. Every

Quaker who speaks at a meeting of friends, is believed to speak under the impulse of inspiration.

Whatever may be the evils of ecclesiastical celibacy—which will be fully displayed in the following pages—it was introduced as one of the essential bases of sacerdotal discipline. It was certainly a bold innovation of the Church to suppress the hereditary priesthoods characteristic of antiquity among the Greeks and Romans, and also with the Jews. Thus, by throwing spiritual dignities open to all ranks of society, a pure theocracy was rendered impracticable, and the medieval Christians were spared the infliction of a Levitical priesthood, and of seeing all pontifical offices of importance the exclusive patrimony of a few privileged families or a certain caste.

A temporal principality was necessary to the European independence of the chief Pontiff. Had the Pope not been a temporal prince, he would have been absorbed by some emperor or king, and the Catholic system, instead of being a propaganda to the world, would have been merely a local establishment like the Anglican, or the Greek church in Russia.

The attribute of general education was an important characteristic of the Catholic system. *Confession* was a necessary complement of education. The directors of youth required this moral influence to enable them to superintend the discharge of the principles they taught. In the same way the principal dogmatic conditions are based on a moral necessity. *Faith* was required to check the discordant expression of the religious spirit. The dogma of the fall and original sin was necessary to explain human suffering, and as a motive for the necessity of a universal redemption. *Purgatory* was a merciful corrective to the doctrine of the eternity of future punishment!

The "Real Presence" gave to the most ordinary priest a daily power of miraculous consecration, making him an object of veneration to great men who cannot aspire to such sublime operations. The Catholic Mass replaced universally and irrevocably the hideous and bloody sacrifices of Polytheism—a sublime subterfuge to satisfy the instinctive demand for sacrifices necessarily inherent in every system of religion, by the voluntary daily immolation of the greatest victim imaginable. Catholicism transformed *slavery* into *serfdom*, interposed between master and slave, the lord and serf, a salutary, spiritual authority, equally respected by both. Catholicism influenced chivalry, and converted a simple means of military education into a powerful instrument of social progress.

The moral and intellectual efficacy of Catholicism were not less than its political wisdom; it consecrated the authority of parents, abolished the almost absolute despotism which it possessed among the ancients, among the Jews, as well as other nations. Catholicism ameliorated the social position of women, and made marriage an indissoluble contract; replaced savage patriotism by the more elevated sentiment of universal humanity, brotherhood, or charity; and was the fruitful source of so many admirable asylums for the relief of human wretchedness.

Its intellectual attributes were apparent; the influence of monotheism as embodied in Catholicism had favoured the progress of the principal natural sciences, chemistry, anatomy, mathematics, and astronomy. Its Æsthetic influence was displayed in the marked encouragement rendered to music, architecture, painting, and sculpture.

CHAPTER V.

THE JESUIT INSTITUTE.

The Catholic system shows an intimate acquaintance with human nature, and the wants and wishes of mankind. It may be pronounced a triumph of human intelligence; in the centuries during which it has been established, it connects and blends together two phases of society utterly at variance with each other—ancient pagan, and modern Christian civilization. Supposing a spectator, utterly unbiassed by prejudices of association and education (an impossibility) to deliberate whether he will be a Catholic or a Protestant, he might embrace the Protestant religion because it seems to be more consistent with liberty of thought and progress, but he must admire Catholicism, so venerable from its age, and the important part it has played in the history of civilization. He cannot consent to look only at the flaws in this wonderful edifice.

It was to save this venerable system from the destruction menaced by the spread of the Reformation that a Spanish hidalgo turned religious enthusiast, founded the Society of Jesus—certainly the most extraordinary fraternity which the world has ever seen. About twenty years after Luther had passed through the mental discipline which resulted in making him the apostle of reformation, Ignatius Loyola was undergoing that spiritual change which converted a fiery soldier, dreaming of crusades, and the conquest of the heathen, to the most ascetic saint, and the founder of an order destined to oppose a barrier to the progress of the innovating doctrines, and even to recover countries which had been lost to the Holy see.

Macaulay writes, " Poor, obscure, without

a patron, without recommendation, he entered the city where now two princely temples, rich with painting, and many-coloured marbles commemorate his great services to the church; where his form stands sculptured in massive silver; where his bones enshrined amidst jewels, are placed beneath the altar of God." No one, I think, who reads the account of Loyola's conversion, can doubt that he was as sincere and conscientious in defending, as Luther was sincere and conscientious in attacking, the doctrines of Rome. In this, indeed, lay the triumph of both. Had Loyola not been sincere, he never would have made disciples of Francis Xavier, Faber, Lainez, and others, to whom he first communicated the idea of his extraordinary society.

If Protestants are not over-willing to examine Catholicism impartially, still less do they regard Jesuitism candidly. The word "Jesuit" is used in an offensive sense, to denote an utter absence of principle, and the most unscrupulous cunning, to attain an end. It is certainly not difficult to make out a bad case for the Jesuits. A society which became so unpopular that its members were expelled from every country of Europe, Catholic, as well as Protestant, and the order finally suppressed by the Pope, could not have been a model of all the cardinal virtues. But it would be unfair and erroneous to rush to the conclusion, as many do, that the society was not originally formed from sublime motives, or that it did not number among its members earnest and good, albeit mistaken, men.

In the progress of this narrative it will be necessary to make some critical remarks on Jesuitism, and to refer to that remarkable book, "Loyola's Spiritual Exercises." At present I shall briefly observe that Jesuitism offers the spectacle presented by so many other societies and fraternities, both political and religious, in which ambitious worldly men of indifferent moral character, frequently climb to the top, or exert great personal influence by the aid of their single-hearted brethren. The peculiar construction of the society of Jesus seems especially to have favoured the display of this feature.

While some cannot believe in a good Jesuit, others are incredulous as to the very existence of the society. They cannot deny that it did exist; but they conceive that it was totally annihilated by the Bull of Pope Clement the Fourteenth, in 1773. It found a refuge in Russia under Catherine then, and it was formally restored by a Bull of Pius the Seventh, in 1814. But even, if it had never been restored, can any one believe that a society which maintained such a formidable ascendancy for 200 years, which actually stemmed the tide of reformation, and regained countries which Popery had lost; which intrigued in every European land, and penetrated into Asia and America; which, through the powerful instrument of the confessional, guided national councils, made and deposed kings, governed and permeated society by the engine of education; that Jesuitism could have been annihilated by a Papal Bull?

But if every Jesuit college and seminary could be closed, we should still find evidences of the society's existence everywhere. Its principles enter more or less into every religion, into every polity. The priest who decrys the use of "human reason" (whatever "human reason" may be) is a Jesuit. Every individual who surrenders the right of private judgment to ecclesiastical authority, is fulfilling the grand principle of the Jesuit's implicit obedience. The complete submission of the individual will to authority, to be as Loyola phrased it, "like a corpse," *perinde ac cadaver*, or a stick in the hand of an old man, is one of the most fundamental features of the Jesuit constitution.

Certainly the priestly influence is very great in the Romish Church; but is it confined to that church? Is it only *there* that the priest attempts to tame man by early education, to conquer him by enlisting the influence of woman? How many clergymen of the High Church party would like to introduce confession into the establishment? But if the confessor is not yet established among us, the spiritual director is, and his influence is even greater than that of the confessor. No form of Protestantism is practically without the spiritual director. He is a more marked feature of dissent than of the establishment. There, the spiritual functions of the clergy, being more definite, do not permit that close and almost daily interference with the laity which we see in other denominations. In Scotland, the personal influence of the clergy is extraordinary, so that we have a remarkable illustration of the saying that "Extremes meet." Exeter Hall and the Tabernacle in England, and Scotland generally, while hating and denouncing Popery, actually copy Popery in this respect—the great personal influence wielded by the clergy and especially with female disciples.

Mrs. Weller, in the "Pickwick Papers," had

her spiritual director in Mr. Stiggins, and amongst Dissenters generally the clergyman wields as much influence as the Catholic priest, though the former may not appear to exert it so directly as the latter.

CHAPTER VI.

"NOLO EPISCOPARI" PRONOUNCED IN EARNEST.

As may be supposed, Father Stirling's reputation was greatly increased by the adventure narrated in the last chapter but two. The Protestant, as well as Catholic papers, paid a deserved compliment to his humanity, moral courage, and Christian charity. Father Stirling was honoured by an interview with the highest dignitary of the Roman Church at that time in England, Archbishop Middleton. This prelate had been selected to fill his responsible station from his moderate views. He was strictly orthodox, but he was not prone to proselytism. He was known to be on terms of friendship with dignitaries of the Anglican Church. In a word, he was a living illustration that a man may fully acknowledge the spiritual supremacy of the Pope, and yet be staunch to his national allegiance and Christian charity.*

The conversation turned upon the Tractarian movement then beginning at Oxford. Father Stirling frankly confessed that his parochial duties left him little time for reading, and that he had not as yet found time to read any of these publications, which had begun to stir ecclesiastical controversy in England.

* "If I knew or believed that the preceding doctrine was opposed to the teaching of the Church, I would, through God's grace, cut out my tongue sooner than utter it, cut off my right hand sooner than write it down, except for the purpose of rejecting it. Let my proposition be submitted to the Holy See, and if the Holy See condemns it, I will not only cheerfully submit; but publish before the world the condemnation, and my unreserved adhesion to it. * * * And now, in concluding this long answer, waiving all question of abstract right, or duty to punish, or to tolerate, from my heart, I wish that all parties, Catholics and Protestants, would agree together that heretics should be coerced only by the force of argument, burned only in the fire of charity, cut off only with the sword of prayer, and all good works; that not only temporal punishments and civil disabilities, except for civil crimes, should be abandoned; but all angry revilings and re riminations, unchristian passions, under the mask of Christian zeal. We can hardly hope for the full accomplishment of this—the devil and the world, and the flesh, are too strong on the other side; but we may strive for it, and approach, though we cannot reach it. For my own part, 'I have faith in my faith,' and I believe that if we tried only the weapons which the Divine founder of Christianity has put into our hands, we would come nearer to a united decision on that great controversy which can never be decided by the arms of worldly warfare."

Extracts from answers of the Rev. P. Murray, D.D., to the Maynooth Commissioners in 1853.

"And of course, your Reverence, refrains from giving an opinion on books you have not read," said Doctor Middleton. "But that is not the case with some of the Anglican clergy. I saw in the paper that a great meeting of divines in the north had been called to protest against the Romish tendencies of these tracts, and it turned out that not one of the persons present at the meeting had read them. Although these writers are very far at present from embracing Catholic truth, it is evident that they are on the right road. I feel confident that these men are coming over to us."

It would be superfluous to tell the intelligent reader that this prediction of the worthy Archbishop was afterwards verified. There is no need to mention here the names of the eminent clergymen who from conscientious motives seceded from the Anglican to the Roman Church.

"But," resumed the archbishop, "your Reverence referred to your parochial duties, demanding all your time, and encroaching on hours of study. That is partly the reason why I desired to see you. Your indefatigable zeal is well known. Doctor Hood assures me that he has frequently, both as a friend and as your ecclesiastical superior advised you to spare yourself, to improve your diet, and give yourself more relaxation; but he has found you obstinate—almost contumacious. What think you then, since the idea your Reverence entertains of parochial duty is to monopolize the work of a dozen priests, there is nothing for it but to relieve you of the duties of a parish priest."

"Pray what may your lordship mean?" said Father Stirling, quite puzzled to understand the archbishop's jocular manner of speaking.

"Why, Mr. Stirling, as you seem so determined not to spare yourself, as you carry works of supererogation to a degree which is injurious to your health, and as your services are so precious to the church, I have recommended you to a preferment, the dignity of which will compel you to take more leisure, while at the same time its duties will amply employ your active mind. I am happy to inform you that I received yesterday a letter from Rome, in which I learn that the Sacred College approves of my recommendation, and that consequently you will be appointed to the first bishopric which becomes vacant in the province under my jurisdiction."

A Catholic bishopric in a Protestant country may not seem a very tempting prize. The actual emolument when compared with that of an Anglican prelacy is indeed small; but let the reader endeavour to put himself in the place of a hard-worked parish-priest, and then imagine what his feelings would be on seeing the mitre and crozier suddenly offered to him. In an ambitious mind what hopes, what dreams would such a preferment awaken! Father Stirling was, in spite of all his virtues, a mere mortal man, subject to all the infirmities of human nature, as his future history will manifest.

What wonder, then, if thus suddenly brought into contact with a high dignitary, who had gratified him by his affability and by that praise which all men love, the natural worldly ambition of the man had been stirred? What wonder if he hesitated as the tempting offer was made to him; that his mental vision was for a moment dazzled by the flashing meteor of imagination? And then he might accept the offer with the purest intentions. To become a bishop, that is overseer, chief pastor in some Catholic community in some remote part of England, Wales, or Ireland: might he not do much more good as a bishop than as a simple priest? But, on the other hand, he might not be appointed to a rural prelacy, and, at any rate, he would possess power and dignity. His position would make him a personage. Pride and worldly feeling might, in spite of himself, spring up in his heart. Could he resist the temptation? He might be thrown into the society of men not given to spiritual longings. What an avenue of temporal ambition might be opened to him!

With the magical quickness of thought, Father Stirling penetrated the imaginary future, revolved the possible events of years in those few moments in which he kept silent. He saw two careers wide and distinct, one humble but virtuous, the other great but worldly, branching off from the decision of that instant, and he wisely returned to his first impulse, which was to decline the Archbishop's offer. Was he right or wrong? The French Satirist says:—

"Distrust first impulses. They are almost always good."

Doctor Middleton, who naturally construed Father Stirling's silence into emotion and inability to express his sentiments of gratitude, and whose features wore the kindly expression of a man who is conscious of conferring a favour on a deserving person, was not a little astonished when the priest replied:—

"I respectfully and sincerely thank your lordship for your good opinion and the signal favour you show me, but I must beg permission to decline the dignity which you offer to my acceptance."

"How! you decline?" said the Archbishop, in a tone of surprise and mortification. "And on what grounds, pray, does your Reverence decline?"

"In the first place, my lord, I feel myself in many respects unworthy of, and incompetent to, discharge the duties of so responsible an office as a bishop. Inclination and duty prompt me to continue in the humbler capacity of a priest where I have tried my strength, and in which I feel my true vocation lies."

Doctor Middleton took a pinch of snuff from a silver box, and said:—

"Your Reverence is indeed worthy of your reputation of singular disinterestedness."

He paused a minute, and then added, in a drier tone:—

"The bishopric, however, is not yet vacant—you may think better of it."

"Rest assured I shall give your lordship the same answer which I now do."

"Well, well, we will see when the time come. You will have leisure to reconsider your decision, and though of course you will be perfectly free to accept or decline, remember that your acceptance of the episcopal office will not only please me, but will conduce to the good of the church."

Within a month the sudden death of Doctor Portman, from apoplexy, left a bishopric vacant; the offer of the Archbishop was renewed, and Father Stirling once more declined it thankfully but firmly. Doctor Middleton even urged it on the priest's acceptance, representing that Father Stirling had by far too humble an opinion of his abilities. At length the Archbishop gave up the point, and said, abruptly:—

"Since you decline yourself, does your

Reverence know anyone who would be a suitable candidate for the vacant mitre ?"

Father Stirling immediately named his most intimate friend, Father Wiley.

"Father Wiley!" repeated Doctor Middleton, in a tone of surprise and even of indignation. "Is it possible you do not know that Father Wiley is a Jesuit?"

Father Stirling intimated that he was aware that Father Wiley was a member of the Society of Jesus, but did not know that he was thereby excluded from becoming a bishop.

But Doctor Middleton was evidently no friend to the Jesuits.

Father Stirling went on to expatiate on Father Wiley's learning, decision of character, capacity for business, strictly moral and exemplary life ; all of which qualities he vouched for from his own personal experience.

While he was speaking thus warmly in

favour of his friend, Dr. Middleton kept his eyes fixed on him, and occasionally arched his eye-brows and raised the corners of his mouth. A physiognomist might have read the expression of the Archbishop's face thus:

"Does he really believe all that he is saying? He does! Then how green he must be."

"Apparently," said the Archbishop, "your Reverence is not acquainted with the rules of the Society of Jesus. By a Papal dispensation members are relieved from the ordinary routine of clerical duty, in order that they may have the more liberty to devote to their own important avocations as Jesuits!"

Father Stirling admitted, in the most naive manner, that he had not studied the constitution or history of the society.

"I thought as much," said Doctor Middleton, drily; and he added, quickly: "I shall not fail to bring under the notice of The Holy Father the very remarkable and singularly disinterested conduct of your Reverence.

Were all the priests under my authority animated with but a tithe of the same zeal, the great Protestant heresy would soon fall before the true Catholic faith."

Here the audience came to an end.

CHAPTER VII.

THE CULMINATING POINT OF SANCTITY.

About the beginning of the year 1841, Father Stirling's reputation for sanctity approached its culminating point. His modesty was continually offended by the tributes to his piety either implied or actually uttered in all sincerity by well-meaning persons. The Archbishop kept his word, and it became generally known that Father Stirling had, from the purest motives, declined the dignity and emolument of the episcopal office; a position which, accompanied by his eloquence and abilities, might have opened a field of ambition tempting by its vastness. Such instances of disinterestedness were more common in the primitive than in the modern history of the church.

Many simply devout people even went so far as to say that such piety and goodness as Father Stirling displayed, were proofs that his mission had been blessed with a special inspiration. The good priest was often addressed, both by his inferiors and equals in social position, with a superstitious deference and respect which pained him deeply.

The good man trembled for his humility. In the book wherein he wrote down the results of his daily self-examination, might be seen such entries as this—

"The enemy of souls assails us in the most insidious manner and from quarters least suspected. Pride, the demon pride, lurks under the guise of humility. I have great need now to guard myself against the imputation of self-righteousness. My stumbling-block, as it appears, lies in the very fact that I have for some years back by God's help done my duty indifferently well. They praise me, they call me pious, good, because I have been enabled to avoid the temptation to become worldly, to fall into deadly sin. I who sin daily in my thoughts—O wretch!—O worm! —know yourself to be full of evil! Re-double your prayers and penances. How truly is it said we are all vain of something. We are actually vain of not being vain. Or we are vain of not being vain of not being vain."

Father Stirling had at this time a strong presentiment of coming disaster, that impression which takes possession of the mind in the midst of happiness and good fortune. Was it possible or probable that his condition of prosperity and credit could continue? Would there not be some terrible reaction? He a pattern-priest—the object of praise and envy—did it not seem probable that he might be on the eve of some horrible backsliding, and that in proportion to his elevation would be the greatness of his downfall.

In order to place a faithful portrait of Father Stirling before my readers, I must anatomize his mental and moral structure; I must briefly sketch some slowly operating changes of thought which had been the results of his ecclesiastical experience. Latterly his mind had not been calm. In the first years of his priestly duties his troubled spirit had found rest (as so many others have) in the reflection that he had placed himself under the authority which he believed to be that which is alone delegated from God, that of Rome. But difficulties had arisen in the discharge of his clerical functions, and suggested doubts which he could not reconcile with his own moral and religious convictions. For though a priest, he was still a man; he still dared to think. He was forbidden to bury children who had not been baptised, or adults who had died impenitent, or suicides. This want of charity is certainly not peculiar to the Church of Rome. Have we not lately heard the spiritual head of the Anglican Church declare from his place in Parliament in reference to this very question of the burial service, that he would place his own private judgment above that of the authority of the church which he is sworn to obey.* How then can judgment be consistently pronounced against Doctor Colenso?

This restriction did not seem to Father Stirling in accordance with either the precepts or example of the Saviour. Daily were the prayers of the Church in request for rich sinners who had lived bad, immoral lives, without openly questioning the sacred dogmas of the faith which they professed but did not practice. Yet to the innocent, unbaptised child, or the conscientious sceptic, Christian burial was refused both by the Roman and Anglican Churches. The assumption im-

* "It will be remembered, indeed it can never be forgotten, that the Primate of England, in his place in the House of Lords, gave his sanction to the refusal to perform the burial service in certain cases for which no exception is made in the Liturgy. To that extent the Archbishop avowed himself non-conformist, though not non-juror. His engagement was to perform all the prescribed offices of the Church, but against one he rebels on the score of an excess of charity he cannot stomach. In his subscription he had accepted and bound himself to the ministration, assented and consented to all in the Book of Common Prayer; but on after thought he makes exceptions not made by the Church, and in effect puts himself above the letter and the spirit of the Church's law. How is this recusancy to be distinguished from Dr. Colenso's non-conformity, and upon what principle is the Bishop of Natal to be called upon to quit the Church that does not equally or more strongly apply to the Archbishop of Canterbury."—The *Examiner*, Nov. 14, 1863.

plied in this refusal, that certain sins are unpardonable; this virtual limitation of the Divine clemency seemed to Father Stirling, when he thought as a man, and not as a priest, to border upon impiety and sacrilege.

He also found increasing difficulty in bringing the fruits of his daily experience into his sermons. He dared not preach from his heart. He dared not display to his congregation human nature, and the world, as he knew them to exist. His intellectual power, his purity of mind, his love of truth made him fret under the conventionalities which fettered him in the pulpit. It would have been some comfort, some alloy to his own sadness if he could have unbosomed his heart of the load of human wretchedness, the perception of which was weighing him down to the earth. He pined to tell complacent worshippers what was the real condition of the poor whom they called their brethren. He desired to show them the hideous ulcers festering under the fair surface of civilisation. But he must not tell rich and fashionable sinners of their pet sins! He must not remind them that they were faring sumptuously every day, and living luxuriously, lavishing wealth on their whims and caprices while their fellow-christians were driven by starvation into sin!

Or if he does speak of these things it must be *gently*, so that he might as well remain silent. Indeed on topics where he felt the necessity of speaking strongly, if at all, he was often compelled to remain silent lest he should go too far; lest his fiery indignation should lead him to tell his wealthy hearers and others who did not hear him, that while assuming the Christian name they were living the pagan life of degenerate Epicureans. Father Stirling received hints from his superiors, hints which he could not neglect, that to preach as he wished to preach, would be to attack the framework and constitution of society, and trench upon socialism; that it would introduce heart-burnings between classes, and would drive the rich and fashionable away from Church.

Then, Father Stirling was not sufficiently severe upon heretics to please the strict portion of his congregation. Though firmly believing in the Catholic doctrines he could not believe that those who had been trained to think differently would be damned,* and his own experience in the great metropolis had impresssd upon his mind, that moral worth and virtue were not monopolized by any sect. Yet he sometimes received hints that his discourses savoured of socinianism; that he did not sufficiently insist upon the great doctrine of faith, but confined himself too closely to upholding the necessity of morality and good works. In vain did the worthy priest appeal to his daily experience

* The Church of Rome appears to be inconsistent here. She declares that out of the pale of her Church no one can be saved. So far the natural conclusion is that all Protestants will be damned. The Anglican Church returns the compliment, and damns all who do not accept the Athanasian creed. Roman Catholic theologians make a distinction between material and formal heretics, *id est*, between those who err blindly from simplicity or want of proper information; and those who pertinaciously maintain error. The great mass of Protestants are thus considered only material heretics, and have, therefore—it is presumed—a chance of salvation!

of life, to the very practice of his censors. "You observe," said he, "Catholics and Protestants of every shade of doctrine, and Jews, all living contentedly, harmoniously, together; all protected by the same laws which are now administered without reference to respective creeds.* You observe these various religionists exchanging the courtesies of life, buying, selling, marrying, engaged together in all the pursuits of business and pleasure. Is it not preposterous to say that each believes his to be the only saving religion; that all his good friends who worship differently are destined to eternal damnation by the God whom John calls "Love?"

These reflections carried Father Stirling still further. He began to doubt if men who could continually cloak their religious prejudices thus in the actual affairs of life, where-

* Father Stirling was not quite right here. Jews have not the same privileges as Christians. Nor is the law just which compels a man, whatever may be his religious scruples, to take an oath in giving evidence, or forfeit his rights as a citizen, in a court of so-called justice!

ever business, profit, or pleasure were at stake, could really believe much one way or the other. Especially as the more he studied human nature, did it seem to him that the conduct of men appeared to be hardly, if at all, actuated by their respective religious beliefs. It is a grave charge brought by Protestants against Catholics that the religion of the latter permits a very dangerous latitude to the conscience; that in consequence of the great stress laid on the virtue of confession and penance, the sinner feels his conscience too rapidly relieved; and that it is thus possible for the same individual to be very immoral and very religious! It might be replied; granted that the Church of Rome lies open to this grave imputation, where is the religion to which it does not in a considerable degree apply? Who does not in some degree verify the poet's satire—

> "Compound for sins they are inclined to,
> By damning those they have no mind to."

Among Protestants as well as Catholics there

are too many who make this shocking compromise with conscience. How terrible is the conviction which forces itself on the observant spectator that men are making of religion a means of soothing instead of awakening conscience; that lulled by the false security inspired by a punctual discharge of religious duties, they spiritually sleep and continue in sin! Father Stirling saw several instances of this, among others the following. He was on one occasion a witness to a lively discussion between two persons; one heterodox and sceptical, the other an orthodox professing member of the Church of England. The latter was addicted to a vice which the world considers venial, but which is classed by the Church among the seven deadly sins. The other, an intimate acquaintance, in the course of argument applied the *argumentum ad hominem* in the most unsparing manner. He said, "How can you reconcile your faith with your absolute want of practice? If you really did believe what you profess—but of course you don't, you only think you believe it—you must be aware that according to your belief you are going headlong to perdition!" "Oh," replied the other, "my faith tells me that it is wicked, but such is the infirmity of human nature, and God is merciful."

Father Stirling began to think that there is often more real faith in a man who abstains from all worship and religious professions, than in the man who can, reeking with pollution, prostrate himself in the temple and rise up justified to himself. No wonder if Father Stirling felt forebodings of a coming storm. It is the condition of the priest to believe, and to pay obedience to authority. Why should he think when the Church thinks for him? The ecclesiastic who thinks for himself must be unhappy.

Father Stirling, like many young priests, had been especially severe upon sexual sin, and inflicted heavy penances before he would grant absolution to offenders. It is necessary to explain this apparent inconsistency in a man so gentle and charitable. Having had the advantage of an extremely moral education, which cultivated the intellect and the spiritual part, at the expense of the animal propensities, and being himself in consequence chaste in mind and body, he could not at first understand, or sympathise in the slightest degree with the temptation to commit this sin. It is invariably the young and untried who are the most unforgiving towards it. For a long time the priest remained conscientiously puzzled at the frequency of this sin, which appeared to him then an illustration of the dogma of the original depravity of man's heart. But with years he became more clear sighted and more indulgent, and in one of his moments of indignant candour, in which he sought to relieve his mind through the pen, he wrote as follows:

"Having had many opportunities in my professional capacity to investigate the causes of incontinence both in men and women, I think myself privileged to offer a brief opinion on the subject. The prevalence of that form of sin which the world calls prostitution and vice, accordingly as it refers to women and men, and which in the earlier days of my ministration seemed so unaccountable, I think I can now trace broadly to a natural instinct unchecked by religion, and fatally encouraged by many artificial circumstances, which are the results of our imperfect social system. Why are the ranks of prostitution recruited chiefly from the lower classes? Because *there* the temptations to incontinence are so much greater, and the protections and safeguards of virtue so much less than elsewhere. Men and women naturally seek each other's society. But in the upper classes these meetings are rendered not only harmless but beneficial. Woman receives mental strength from contact with the masculine intellect. The rugged character of a man is softened and elevated by impact with the gentler and more religious spirit of woman. The powerful instincts of nature are held in check by moral and religious training, by a cultivation which diverts the mind, by pride or fear of the world, by restraints of all kinds, which, whether intrinsically noble or ignoble, tend to good. Lastly, among the upper and middle classes there is not the curse of poverty to deaden virtuous resolutions, to thrust the tempted into sin.

But in the humbler ranks of life how different! There, the moral, intellectual, and religious training is very imperfect; the personal pride and fear of the world proportionately weak—in some instances null—and then to aid all these negative inducements to sin there is—oh, how often—the positive crushing tempter—Want! Want of everything which can make life desirable or worthy, and lastly physical want, want of food. 'How strange is human pride!' Why should the rich and noble despise the poor? It is true in the higher and middle ranks of life there is more actual chastity; but what is the distinction in the eyes of the moralist and philosopher? A rich lady buys, a poor lady sells herself to, a husband. The traffic is carried on in drawing-rooms and palaces. The poor woman in humble life, urged by the same love of pleasure, depressed by poverty, falls, and becomes a huckster of an inferior grade, who trades in the streets. Unpitying man derides and scorns. What will be the judgment of the Eternal Father? Perhaps the peeress may be rejected, while the persecuted sinner is clothed in a robe of celestial purity.

But that which most of all disturbed Father Stirling's conscience, that which most of all tortured him, and caused a tumult of revolt in his mind, was the hateful, the awful experience of The Confessional. In vain he tried to look at this powerful machine of medieval invention* as he *had* beheld it, an admirable institution for restraining sin, and lightening the overburthened conscience of the sinner. That

* Auricular confession was first authoritatively established A.D. 1215. —See Neander's Church History, vol. vii. p 491.

was the theory, but the practice, how different! In the first place it burthened him with terrible secrets affecting the welfare of individuals and families; secrets which his priestly oath forbade him to reveal, although the awful responsibility of knowing them weighed the possessor to the earth, saddened his spirit, and seemed to cast a pall over the face of creation, by the hideous crimes revealed in human nature and society.

That the reader may not deem these words at random, I will give the following brief description of a confession to which Father Stirling had once to listen:

A father of a family of four children, a gentleman in decayed circumstances, too proud to apply to the parish for relief, was at length reduced to such destitution that his children were crying for bread. He sent one of them to the baker's to ask for a loaf on credit. The baker refused the loaf on trust. The father in a fit of frantic fury first drowned his youngest and favourite child in the water-butt, as being the easiest death, then cut the throats of the rest, and ended by committing suicide. His wife, half-murdered, succeeded in making her escape, and it was from the lips of this unfortunate woman that the priest heard under the seal of confession the above tragic-tale.

But that ordeal of the confessional which is the most trying to the celibate priest—to confess young, beautiful women of the world—I shall not dwell upon here, as I shall have occasion to illustrate it in the course of the narrative.

CHAPTER VIII.

THE PRIEST IN SOCIETY.

As Father Stirling's health had been failing for some months, his ecclesiastical superior had at length compelled him temporarily to relinquish preaching and other parochial duties; to allow himself a more generous diet, and a few of the relaxations of society But in acting on this advice fresh temptations lay in weight for the unfortunate priest. As an ecclesiastic he was believed to be superior to human weaknesses! His great reputation for piety had surrounded him with a halo of sanctity which amounted almost to the ascription of infallibility. His presence at an evening party created a sensation. All were interested in observing the celebrated preacher,

—the good, humble parish priest, who had declined a bishopric. Women, of course, half-worshipped him. They adore priests and soldiers! On these occasions Father Stirling was generally surrounded by a circle of female devotees—lovely women, in all the bewitching *abandon* of full dress evening toilet. These beautiful creatures, believing him to be an anchorite, a man above human passions, innocently vied with each other which could render him most attention. Reposing perfect confidence in his sacred office, in the sainted purity of his character, they treated Father Stirling with an intoxicating familiarity; they hung upon his words while the speaker could not avoid inhaling the perfume emanating from their glossy hair; could even, at times, feel their breath fanning his cheeks. Men have had the moral courage to refrain from placing themselves within the sphere of woman's influence, but no man who has undergone the peril could ever resist the adorable flattery of beauty.

At first Father Stirling manfully withstood this novel trial. Nay, as a modest man and an ascetic, his delicacy and taste were offended at the spectacle presented by women in full dress, and engaging in dances which, to an inexperienced spectator, appear like wrestling-matches! Be it remembered that this simple man had not had his æsthetic tastes developed by assisting at the representation of a ballet. It is no wonder then if the female full dress costume of good society struck him as being improper and contrary to real purity of heart. This unworldly and eccentric man thought he could discern in it an insidious attempt to attract and vanquish men, through an appeal to their animal passions. He would even have preached against it, but he was warned that he had better avoid the subject; for that, if he once offended the ladies by attacking so time-honoured a custom as the liberal display of their charms in full dress his popularity as a preacher would at once decline.

Wonderful is the power of habit. Though the priest's reason was still unconvinced he became reconciled to low, evening dresses. Gradually he felt a strange and novel pleasure stealing over him in the society of women at large parties.

At length this intoxication of the senses, aided and abetted by the more liberal diet which he allowed himself, began seriously to alarm Father Stirling for his purity. Instead of beholding as formerly in his dreams the countenance of the blessed Virgin, after Murillo (a copy of which exquisite picture hung in his room), he saw the lovely faces and languishing looks of the beautiful women he had met in society. He became suddenly alive to the danger which menaced him, and battled against it with all the means at his disposal. He arose in the silent watches of the night, and passed hours in prayer or silent contemplation, kneeling in the cold, and on the bare floor before the picture of the Madonna. While thus engaged, under the dim light of a lamp which was pendent from the ceiling, he would have formed a fine subject for the pencil of Corregio or Rembrandt. The Priest endeavoured by maceration and other severe penances to impose silence on what he then believed to be the temptations of the devil. For he believed himself to be undergoing the same ordeal as St. Anthony. He believed that religion could and would enable him to conquer the strongest instincts of Nature.

Yet this man had begun to think, and there were times when he asked himself why Nature and Religion should thus be at strife? The voice of Reason would make itself heard. And on these occasions the unhappy man would exclaim, in the solitude of his chamber: "Is it my fault, if I make use of the perception and the senses God has given me, to see and admire the beauty which He has so lavishly bestowed on women? Were they then not meant to be admired? Yes; but not by me. By my vows I am as one dead —to the world—to human passions—to the very perception of beauty in its highest form. I may admire a fragrant flower—a beautiful picture—but not a beautiful woman. Why then can I not stifle these feelings?" There were two answers to the question. Religion prompted the reply: "Because I am a sinner; because I have not sufficiently weaned my heart from carnal lusts. And it is necessary for my salvation that I should undergo this temptation—that my soul may issue refined and purified from the ordeal." Reason said: "Because you are a man—a young man. The word priest signifies an old man, and the office of a priest is incompatible with youth."

Such were the strange and bitter revulsions of feeling going on in the mind of Father Stirling, as he went into society and made acquaintance with his fellow-beings and human nature, not through a conventional and sacerdotal medium, but through the equality of social relations. He beheld the grand and wonderful panorama of Life passing before his eyes.

The spectacle was novel, and interested him. He witnessed the thrillng drama with its scenes of inextricably interwoven and blended pleasure, pain, innocence, and guilt—forming a moral problem which no human judgment is competent to solve. He saw its ambitions, loves, hates, fears, its thousand departments of action, feeling, enjoyment, industry, worthy and unworthy employment. He felt like a spectator for ever debarred from becoming an actor. To fill this negative condition contentedly, a man's will must be of colossal dimensions. His sacred profession imposed upon him the assumption that he was quite indifferent to the busy world. Yet his conscience whispered to him that such was not the case. Gradually an uneasy idea had been growing up in his mind that he had been cajoled, cheated, duped, and deceived; that he had made a grand mistake at the very outset of his career; that both by natural inclination, by ability, and social position, he was fitted to play a part very different from that of a priest, on the stage of life.

As usual, in all difficulties, he sought counsel from his intimate friend Father Wiley. The latter appeared to sympathise sincerely with Father Stirling's sufferings; assured him that they were only trials sent to prove his faith; that his experience was by no means singular; that he was only passing through the fiery ordeal from which he would issue like refined gold from the furnace. When the young priest proposed flying society altogether, and taking refuge in solitary studies and his parochial duties, as the best or only antidotes to the worldly poison which he felt to be corrupting his soul, the Jesuit strenuously but artfully dissuaded him from taking any such step, and assured him that the best way was to face the world, the flesh, and the devil; that if the spiritual warrior resolutely made up his mind to conquer, victory was certain, etc.

Father Stirling, relying on his own strength, his own piety, followed this advice. He said to himself; "Virtue does not consist in shunning, but in overcoming temptation. I will conquer the world, the flesh, and the devil!" he exclaimed, and vanity whispered to him: "Are you not the pious, the holy father Clement?" He knew not the divided allegiance of his adviser. Father Wiley loved Father Clement as far as he (the slave of an authority which used him as its tool) was permitted to love anything or anybody. The single-minded priest knew not the insidious nature of the temptation in store for him.

Still acting under medical and ecclesiast advice Father Stirling went more than (into society. Under the excusable plea of restoring his constitution, impaired by overduty, midnight vigils, penance, and ascetic living, he put to the proof the truth of the adage, that it is difficult to touch pitch without being defiled. He, who had formerly made religion the sole aim of life, now reluctantly compromised with the world. He conversed with men who made no secret of their devotion to gallantry, pleasure, or inordinate pursuit of wealth. He feasted his eyes on the beauty of women; regaled his ears with their syren tones; treasured in his heart the subtle flattery which they throw into the simplest glance or gesture. He became courtly in his manner, which had previously been, in spite of his natural charity, occasionally *brusque*, harsh, and offensive. He studied the art of conversation and endeavoured to reply to the lively sallies of witty and accomplished women.

Though he sank in his own estimation when he had the courage to examine himself strictly, Father Stirling became infinitely more popular in society and especially with the ladies. It must be confessed that it is exceedingly difficult for an ecclesiastic (especially if he is popular) to trace a satisfactory plan for his behaviour in the world. He is tolerably certain to end in practically illustrating the fable of the old man and his sons taking the ass to market. By trying to please everybody he will please none. If he refuse to unbend, he is voted "churlish" and "a bore" in society. If on the other hand he tries to be "all things to all men," those who are most ready to avail themselves of his complaisance in society, will often be the first to accuse him, behind his back, of conduct unseemly in a clergyman. But amongst his own religionists there seemed not a dissenting voice to mar Father Stirling's popularity. When he softened the austerity of his demeanour; when he consented to talk the language of the world, it was deemed a singular condescension on the part of so holy a man. The most delicious flattery a superior man can bestow on society, is to enter into its frivolous amusements. And then pious people lay the flattering unction to their souls, that those relaxations, festivities, and pleasures in which the clergy share, cannot be reprehensible. It is all the same whether the scene is laid in ducal or princely halls—where plump and courtly bishops consecrate the revel—or at a dissenters' tea-meeting, where the great popular preacher, in the intervals of praying and singing hymns, makes the delighted assembly roar with laughter. Human nature is everywhere the same: men and women are glad to forget for a time their spiritual attitudinizing and become happy.

Hitherto I have painted the bright and palmy view of Father Stirling's priestly career. Now, I enter upon another and more gloomy phase of the picture. Now, it is my painful duty to exhibit this noble nature assailed with doubts, tormented with the most irresistible temptations, and weighed down to the earth with a burthen of anguish almost too heavy for the human soul to bear.

BOOK III.

CHAPTER I.

MADELINE'S CONSTANCY.

IT was in the beginning of 1842, when Father Stirling was present at a large evening entertainment, at the same house whence about two years ago he had been summoned to attend the condemned felon in Newgate. The hostess, Lady Oldtowers, has already been introduced to the reader. She was a woman of forty, still beautiful, and not a little vain of her position in the fashionable world. Her rank and wealth made her an important member of the Catholic community; and as such, Father Stirling had received an intimation from ecclesiastical authority that she was to be treated with marked consideration. In endeavouring to carry out these instructions the priest had to struggle between inclination and duty. The more he saw of Lady Oldtowers' private character the less he liked her. On after reflection he had been a good deal shocked by her unfeeling remark on the occasion of his visit to Newgate. Seldom indeed did he converse with the lady without hearing something which pained his conscientious convictions. On this evening, while discussing some religious topic, she said, abruptly:—

"One does not wish to be uncharitable, but I cannot shut my eyes to the wickedness of the world. Look at this great country, still persevering, still glorying in its heresy. It is very sad to be obliged to say so, but when I look around me I am forced to think of that remarkable passage in Massillon's eloquent sermon on the exceedingly small number of the elect. I am afraid, your Reverence, that the great majority of people are wilfully taking the downward road which leads to perdition. Pray what does your reverence think?"

Father Stirling did not answer the question. He immediately diverted the conversation into another channel, and was not sorry when Lady Oldtowers, turning to speak to another lady, gave him an opportunity of ending their dialogue. Her last words seemed revolting, both in themselves and from the manner in which they were spoken. Here was a lady, lapped in luxury, passing easily and graciously through life—that tragic drama or prosaic struggle to so many—apathetically declaring her belief in the probable perdition of the great majority of her fellow species!

The religion of Lady Oldtowers dwelt more in externals than internals; she came to church in all her worldly bravery, her temporal panoply; she fell into a delicious intoxication of the spirit while listening to the music of the mass; her feelings were not unfrequently wrought up till they found vent in tears; and what was the result of all this piety of the senses? Once outside the walls of the church, she belonged again to the world. Nay, after her periodical confessions, she returned to her life of gaiety, frivolity, and folly, with infinitely greater zest, as though she had wiped off the balance of her sins, and could now, with a safe conscience, begin again. Thus her religion was like her banker's book. She kept a debtor and creditor account with heaven, and doubtless believing herself good—both in the spiritual and commercial sense—sometimes felt herself at liberty to overdraw her account, and sin a little in advance.

She would put down her name to an ostentatious charity for a sum which, however large in itself, caused the donor no real deprivation; but to superintend the disposal of her own bounty, to impose on herself the duty of seeking out real objects of pity, and verifying the fact of real pressing necessity, which indiscriminate alms-giving never reaches—this was a labour for which her ladyship had neither time nor inclination. How, indeed, can the rich sympathise with the poor? Sitting in her chariot, she saw not the beggar-woman pressing her starved child to her withered bosom; and as for some forms of misery, her ladyship's prudery would have taken mortal offence at the bare mention of them. Nothing must be said in her virtuous presence about "fallen" women. She ignored their very existence. There is an intimate connection between the heart and the optical nerve requisite to see certain sorrows. In spite of the streets swarming with prostitution, and the revelations of the divorce-court, a fiction must be kept up that *all* women are virtuous.

Father Stirling had already made wonderful progress in the teaching of the world. Although indignant at the narrow and uncharitable views expressed by Lady Oldtowers, he hid his feelings under the unmeaning, stereotyped smile which he saw on the faces of others. When it was possible—that is, when her remarks did not altogether outrage his moral sense—he replied with a bow, and allowed her to imagine that he acquiesced in her sweeping censure. Meanwhile he regarded the lively scene displayed by the ball-room with a bland and placid countenance which concealed the real bitterness at heart. A civil discord was raging in his mental kingdom, which might be expressed by the following soliloquy:

"What right have I to disdain those whom I see laughing, chattering, grimacing around me? Yet how inconsistent do these frivolous occupations — singing, dancing, flattering, eating sumptuous fare, and drinking generous wines — appear with their belief as Christians in an eternal destiny of joy or woe—with the doctrine that this earth is only a temporary halting-place, a preparatory stage in the journey to salvation! Viewed only from the lower sense of morality, it is wrong, for while these rich sinners are thus amusing themselves in this lavish profusion, there are now, in this mighty city, hundreds and thousands who are suffering, and slowly dying for want of the necessaries of life—their fellow-species—their brethren in Christ! Yet, if these thoughtless revelers are wrong, how much more criminal am I—*I*, a labourer in the Lord's vineyard, a priest, a preacher of the gospel, a teacher of the precepts of Christ—*I*, who should be an example and a beacon-light! Why, I am a hundred fold more sinful than others, for my very presence here is accepted by many as a guarantee that they may, with a safe conscience, indulge in the pleasures of the world. Thus I, the shepherd, allure the flock to destruction."

The complexion of his thoughts assumed a more cheerful hue. "Are they right, after all? Is it merely a harmless amusement, thoroughly consistent with religious professions? Why, then, can I not be an actor as well as a spectator? Why is the dance prohibited to me? I am neither old, nor ugly, nor deformed. On every side I behold smiling, joyous faces; young men and maidens pressing each other's hands as they pass in the mazes of the dance, or whispering honied words which cause eyes to sparkle, cheeks to colour, while their guardians and parents look on approvingly. Why must I alone affect an indifference to beauty, a superiority to pleasure, a stoical equanimity which I am far from feeling?"

At this stage of his soliloquy, Father Stirling's attention was attracted by the conversation of two ladies who sat at a little distance before him, and who were evidently discussing some other lady, who, from the position in which he stood—a curtained alcove—was invisible to him.

"Do you think her so very handsome, Priscilla, as she is said to be?"

"I can't say that I do, as far as I can

judge from this distance; but the gentlemen appear to be bewitched by her; only see how they are crowding around her."

"Yes; that is the way with the men; let a woman once get a little reputation for beauty, and they all run after her just like a flock of geese. She is as pale as the lilies in her hair, and totally without animation. One might as well admire a beautiful statue. I confess I am quite disappointed, for I had heard so much of her beauty, that I came to-night full of curiosity to see her. And then, she is a *blonde*—a style of beauty which I never could admire."

The speaker was a brunette, with an extremely florid complexion.

"It is her history, Julia, which makes her so interesting. I have heard it from Mrs. Chatterly, who made me acquainted with her some time since."

"An affair of the heart, I presume? the old story of disappointed love?"

"You speak of these things with sad

levity, Julia," said the other lady, in a demure tone. "You are right; but in this case the incidents are somewhat singular, and unusually affecting."

"You quite rouse my curiosity; pray let me hear this pathetic history."

"About eight or nine years ago, she was engaged to be married; Mrs. Chatterly did not know the gentleman's name; I believe they had been betrothed as children; it was quite an eligible match—both equal in rank and fortune—and a pure matter of affection. Well, it appears that just when everything was settled—I think Mrs. Chatterly said the very day for the ceremony was appointed—"

"The lover died?"

"No."

"Proved recreant?"

"No; he was discovered to have joined the Catholic church."

Here the speaker devoutly touched a small ornament, in the shape of a cross, which she wore suspended from her neck.

"Was that all? Did that break off the match?"

"You may well ask, Julia. Her father was an obstinate heretic—"

"Thank you," said Julia, with vivacity.

"I beg your pardon, Julia," returned the other; "I had no intention of wounding your feelings; I meant to say her father was peculiarly strict in his religious convictions, and a member of the Anglican church. He professed to be shocked at the duplicity of the lover in concealing the change in his religious opinions, though I think he had himself to blame for that, for had he been more tolerant, the lover would probably not have feared to state that he was a Catholic. At any rate the father forbad his daughter to marry; and she, from a sense of duty, sacrificed herself. She must have loved him deeply, for it appears she has never rallied from the blow of separation. Her father, who doats on her, has tried every possible means to bring about her recovery, both of mind and body. They have been abroad for years—in Italy, residing in Naples, Rome, Florence—in short—all over Europe, and I believe they went as far as Egypt. But it appears no change of scene will avert her melancholy, or reinstate her health. She has been presented at Court; she is known to be an heiress; she has received many eligible offers, and there is a gentleman now present whom her father wishes her to marry. It is said that she hates society, but that she goes out merely to comply with her father's wishes, and pretends to be enjoying herself, while her heart is broken."

"Poor creature! Her story is exactly like a romance. It puts me in mind of those beautiful lines written by Moore, on the young lady who died broken-hearted on account of her love for that unfortunate character—Emmett—'She is far from the land where her young hero sleeps.'"

"I think so too. Perhaps I may have it in my power to bring some consolation to her, for she is evidently only a *material*, not a *formal* heretic."

"Really I had begun to think that real disinterested love was only to be met with in novels. I shall have a better opinion of the world—at least of my own sex? And the lover—what became of him. I suppose he forgot her, and is now comfortably married?"

"No! It is said he took the blow so deeply to heart that he retired from the world."

"You don't mean destroyed himself?"

"Oh, no! He sought, and doubtless has found, consolation where alone is to be found a refuge in affliction—in religion! He entered into Holy Orders. He became a priest."

"Did he go into a convent—I mean a monastery?"

"I don't know. Mrs. Chatterly said he became a priest."

"He ought to have become a monk. It

would have made the story so much more romantic, you know."

"Oh, Julia, what levity on such a sad subject."

Father Stirling's heart beat faster and faster as he listened to this story so closely resembling his own history. No names had been mentioned, and as he remained under the conviction that Madeline Singleton had married many years ago, he began to think that the tale he had just heard only embodied a strange coincidence of events. He waited in the hope that one or other of the speakers would mention the name of the lady who formed the subject of their discourse. In this expectation he was disappointed. They suddenly changed the conversation, and began talking, by another strange coincidence, of—*himself.*

"I am so glad you agree with me in thinking that the health of His Reverence Father Stirling is so much improved."

"Oh, very much. I never before saw him looking so well as he is to-night. I had begun to fear that his lungs were affected."

"Ah, yes; that was the danger. Preaching so often as he did. That is the misfortune of being so gifted. The eloquent preacher runs the risk of destroying his own life while employed in saving souls. And then he did so much parochial duty besides—visiting, and other works of supererogation. I am so glad that he has at last thought proper to give himself some relaxation. He will soon get completely well, now that he goes so much more into society than he did. And then the happiness which his presence conveys to others. I declare the very sight of his calm, intellectual features does me good, whether I have an opportunity of hearing him speak or not. And then the contrast between the habitual grave, almost melancholy, expression—and his remarkably sweet smile—"

"He is certainly a most eloquent preacher.

You know how pleased I was when I went, at your request, to hear him."

"Oh! as a preacher there is no one to compare with him; but if you knew his private character as well as I do, Julia, you would not wonder at the universal esteem which he inspires."

"It was highly creditable to him to refuse the offer of a bishopric. It proves that his heart is not set upon temporal things."

"I do love to hear him praised by the heretics—excuse me, Julia—the Protestants—but I can assure you his refusal of the bishopric was nothing extraordinary for him, and required no particular or special act of self-sacrifice. It was simply in accordance with the whole tenor of his life."

Father Stirling, thus compelled to hear his own praises, formed an exception to the rule that listeners never hear good of themselves. He was watching for an opportunity to escape from a somewhat equivocal position, and also to satisfy his curiosity as to the identity of the lady who had formed the subject of the previous conversation, when a parting in the crowd enabled him to catch a glimpse of the person in question.

"Oh, look, Julia; she is standing up to dance in the next set of quadrilles. How frail and delicate she looks. Do you know who that officer, her partner, is?"

"Yes! Major Darton."

"Major Darton! why that is the name Mrs. Chatterly mentioned. That must be the gentleman her father wishes her to marry."

As the lady took her place in a set of quadrilles on the opposite side of the room, Father Stirling involuntarily pressed forward, unconscious and regardless of the exclamation of astonishment which burst from the two ladies on recognizing him. He still kept advancing, with his eyes steadily fixed on the lady, whom, in spite of the great change wrought by nine years of affliction, he recognized as the still beautiful Madeline Singleton!

He saw not, he heeded not the dancers who

occupied the floor in momentary expectation of the commencement of the music. Place, circumstances, the moral chasm which separated him from Madeline, all things were forgotten in one overwhelming tide of memory called up by this most unexpected meeting. He kept advancing as if drawn by a magnetic influence towards that fair delicate woman. Madeline raised her eyes, saw, and recognised her old lover in Father Stirling! At that instant the band struck up a most lively set of quadrilles. A moment before all had been impatient expectation. Gentlemen had been fidgetting with their kid gloves, settling their collars, and getting everything in readiness for the solemn act of social pleasure in which they were about to engage. They were preparing, as the French traveller said, to enjoy themselves sadly, after the manner of their country. The ladies had not exhibited any signs of trepidation or nervousness. They never do. But more than one satin-slippered little foot had begun to beat a gentle tattoo on the well-chalked floor. Now, in spite of the lively strains, the dance did not go on. The music ceased. All was commotion and confusion; ladies darted toward one spot with their smelling-bottles. Presently the crowd divided, and Major Darton, carrying the lovely and inanimate form of Miss Singleton, passed out of the heated dancing-rooms.

CHAPTER II.

FATHER WILEY'S HOLY POVERTY.

WHEN Father Stirling found himself in the solitude of his chamber that night, he was utterly unable to yield his mind to his wonted religious exercises, so absorbing was the effect of the discovery he had made. Madeline Singleton still free, still remembering, perhaps still loving him, and pining away in celibacy for his sake! Madeline, whom he had thought heartless and inconstant; Madeline, whom he had striven to banish from his recollection by eight years of (until quite recently) unremitting religious zeal, and Madeline might have been, ought to have been, his wife. How did he know but that when her father perceived her fixed partiality for him, Colonel Singleton might have relented and given his consent to the union rather than see his child die? Why had he been so precipitate as thus to place with his own hand an insurmountable barrier between Madeline and himself? In vain the unfortunate man tried to check the delirium of fancy by striving to recall his religious obligations, that he had vowed himself to God. He could not check the train of his ideas; he could not diminish the poignancy of his regrets, heightened and strengthened as they were by his recent participation in the pleasures of society. He could not pray. More than once, from the force of habit, he threw himself on his knees before the picture of the Madonna; but he saw there no longer the sublime and celestial countenance of "the Immaculate Virgin," * but the image which had burnt itself into his mind—Madeline—as she recognized him—Madeline, as she was borne fainting from the room. He started to

* In the year 1854 the Pope issued a Bull in which the Immaculate Conception of the Virgin—that is, that she was born free from all original sin—was decreed an article of faith.

his feet, and passed the night pacing his chamber. "*Cucullus non facit monachum*"—the priest was absorbed in the man!

On the morrow he sought Father Wiley, both in the capacity of confessor and friend; told him all, and thereby greatly relieved his mind. Father Wiley granted him absolution and imposed a much lighter penance than Father Stirling expected or wished, for the unsettled state of his mind and his growing taste for society seemed to him heinous sins.

"And now, my dear Stirling, what do you propose doing with yourself to-day?"

"I will go and see some of my poor pensioners," replied Father Stirling. "That will divert my mind, and keep me from thinking too much on one subject."

"Indeed, my dear Stirling, you will do nothing of the sort. Your housekeeper can distribute your charities, and you are plainly not in a condition for duty. I impose on you then the penance of dining with me to-day. You must make that self-sacrifice, even if you exclaim with Marcus Aurelius—'I have lost a day.'"

Father Stirling permitted himself to be persuaded. He felt particularly pleased to be with his friend on the present occasion, that he might revert directly or indirectly to the subject which occupied his thoughts. The Jesuit doubtless divined this very natural sentiment. Father Wiley resided at Haverstock Hill. His style of living formed a complete contrast to that of Father Stirling. The house itself was of moderate proportions such as any middle-aged bachelor in easy circumstances might have occupied. But the discerning visitor no sooner entered than he perceived that it was the abode of a man of refined and luxurious tastes. It was furnished throughout with quiet elegance, and if there was a lavish profusion, it was of that kind which is most excusable—that is, objects which contribute to mental rather than bodily comforts—such as books, pictures, statues, busts, vases,

&c. A scrutinizing observer, who gathers shrewdly from all these mute witnesses the character of the possessor, might have said, "This is neither the house of a bachelor nor a married man. The presiding neatness of a woman is displayed, but not that decisive feminine control which marks the presence of *a wife*, who is determined to reduce to practice that clause in the marriage ceremony which endows her with all her husband's worldly goods."

Doubtless the clause sounds well ; only, unfortunately, the practical effect of marriage is just the reverse. The husband takes all the worldly goods of his wife instead of endowing her with his. However, it must be gratifying to all admirers of the beautiful sex to know that women are now "wide awake," and generally take care to settle their property on themselves before marriage, to the great disgust of fortune-hunters.

In short, this tenement gave ample evidence

to the initiated that it was the house of a priest—a priest whose housekeeper was not an old woman. Father Wiley's Lares and Penates were presided over by a young female, whom he had introduced to Father Stirling as an orphan ward and distant relative of his own. This young person was not often seen by visitors. She was excessively timid and retiring, blushing when looked at, never speaking unless addressed, and then in low tones and with a nervous manner. Father Stirling had at first mentally condemned his friend's luxurious style of living as unsuitable to an ecclesiastic; but lately he had grown more lenient in his judgment, and then it was exceedingly difficult to resist the charm of Father Wiley's manner when he was bent on pleasing.

Though not curious, Father Stirling had sometimes wondered how his friend found the means to live so expensively, for he knew him to have no patrimony. He might also have wondered how Father Wiley reconciled this luxury with his Jesuitical vow of poverty.* Father Stirling had of course never touched on so delicate a subject; although the Jesuit had read his thoughts, and had indeed on more than one occasion seemed eager to court enquiry, alluding to his position by vague and general remarks, tending to convey the impression that these worldly goods were not his own, but merely held in trust for the society of which he was a member. Be this as it may, priests like Father Wiley, who direct rich widows and confess wealthy penitents, and have the care of dying worldlings, who cannot carry their wealth into the other

* "Further, it was a fundamental principle with the society that the members were to renounce all secular ties, and to devote themselves to spiritual duties alone. How had not this principle been maintained at other times with such strictness that every entrant renounced his whole property! First, that step was delayed for a while; it was then taken indeed, but only conditionally, inasmuch as the member possibly might be expelled; at length the practice was introduced of members transferring their property to the society: it being clearly understood, however, that this transference should be made to the precise college which each severally entered, in such wise that a man even retained the management of his property after having thus transferred it, only under another title. The members of colleges here and there, having more time at their command than their relations who lived in the midst of society, managed the affairs of the latter, collected their money, and conducted their law-suits. * * * * * *

"It had always remained a fundamental principle, that instruction should be given gratuitously. But presents were taken of receiving pupils, and also on the occasion of particular holidays, which occurred several times in the year: scholars possessed of property were in special request."—Ranke's *Popes of Rome.*

world, have ample opportunities to amass money if so disposed.

Father Wiley was a decided *bon vivant.* Like " the monks of old " he loved good cheer. He was no Trappist. Well, there is no harm in this. Most of our worthy orthodox clergymen believe it possible to make the best of both worlds; and to grow fat is the sign of a good conscience. For my own part I like to see a plump rubicund dean or bishop. Such appears to me a practical illustration of the temporal blessings of piety; and it is extremely gratifying to every philanthropist to know that ecclesiastics can grow fat in spite of such weighty responsibilities. Like Cæsar I say—

> "Let me have men about me that are fat;
> Sleek-headed men, and such as sleep o' nights."

And if heretics may indulge in the pleasures of the table, why not Catholic priests? I have known many fat priests, and I have a theory on that point. Where a man is restrained from marrying and having a family, he naturally likes to compensate himself in some way. Hence the priest, who is true to his vows, and is debarred from the sweetest enjoyment of life—a woman's love—"takes it out" in good living. Who can read without being interested, Mr. Lever's graphic portrait of Father Tom, the worthy Irish priest, who never neglected his religious duties, but who loved "poteen," and occasionally made a bet!

Father Stirling generally made good cheer when he dined with Father Wiley. On the present occasion, however, the guest did not do justice to the appetizing viands with which the table was spread. He neither obeyed the precept nor followed the example of Father Wiley, who pressed him to eat, and ate himself, of soup, fish, joint, *entrées*, &c., while Father Stirling ate but sparingly of one dish, and drank but one glass of wine. The repast being concluded, a Latin grace was said, and the cloth was withdrawn.

"And now, my dear Stirling," said Wiley, as he sipped his wine at dessert, "let us be sociable. I have filled your glass, but you do not drink it. Let us speak together in all confidence. Quite independently of what you have told me to-day, I have seen for some time past that your mind has not been quite at ease, and it has given me pain as well as surprise, for I said to myself, 'surely if any one should have a conscience at rest it ought to be yourself.' I am, as you perceive, a *virtuoso*, a carer for many things, and no despiser of the creature-comforts of this world. I am, I may as well own it, a *gourmand*, and a *gourmet*. I agree with Iago, 'Wine is a good familiar creature,' and also with the wisest of men, 'Wine gladdeneth the heart of a man.' I confess my failings to you, I detest hypocrisy. But you, a pattern, an example, a bright and shining light, our *dulce decus*, you who have really nothing to reproach yourself with—"

"Wiley! no flattery," exclaimed Stirling, abruptly.

"Flattery! Do you think me capable of it?" returned Wiley, as if hurt at the imputation.

"Have I not confessed to you a decay of zeal, a hankering after worldly pleasures, an unsettled mind, dark and gloomy imaginings almost amounting to impious doubts? What business had I at that fatal party where I saw Madeline—Miss Singleton, I mean?"

The penetrating Wiley saw at once that his friend wished to find an excuse for dwelling on the topic which engrossed his thoughts, and he undertook to aid him in the task of self-justification with all his characteristic cunning.

"You deem it, then, a great misfortune to learn that the woman who loved you when you were still in the world, has not forgotten you—will not marry another. After all, as a student of the human heart, you should be pleased to know that there is such a thing to be met with as constancy in woman."

Father Stirling cast a hasty glance at the speaker, who appeared to be uttering his opinion in earnest. If he spoke in irony it was impossible to detect it. The younger priest replied:—

"How can I regard the matter from this abstract point of view? It is true all is for ever at an end between Mad— Miss Singleton and myself. But can I banish memory? Can I forget the tender relations which once existed between us? Oh! no, my friend, it is impossible. Like Macduff,—

> 'I cannot but remember such things were,
> That were most precious to me.'

Ah! Wiley, you cannot see with my eyes or feel with my heart. You are cold because you have never loved."

Had the speaker been less absorbed in his own thoughts he might have noticed a momentary light in Father Wiley's eyes and a strange smile playing over his lips. But his face soon resumed its natural expression as Father Stirling continued.

"Is it not pitiful to think that this woman has been slowly pining away for nine years, while I have been comparatively happy. If she should die I shall feel like a murderer. Have I not caused her death?"

"Certainly not," replied Father Wiley, "for she refused you, happily for you; happily for the interests of the Faith in this heretical country; happily it may be for herself."

"What do you mean, Wiley?"

"After all, this may prove providential. You know how greatly you suffered when the engagement was broken off. Yet you say you have been comparatively happy for years. And why? Because you have been doing good. Because all your energies have been devoted to the highest pursuit in the world — spreading a knowledge of the true faith. How otherwise could you have succeeded in achieving so soon so great a reputation? Why is Miss Singleton not happy? Because she is without the spiritual consolation which attends the profession of the true faith. In the bosom of the Church she would have known peace and resignation."

Father Stirling seemed struck with this idea, and Wiley proceeded.

"What if I were to tell you more; that Miss Singleton's illness is not attributable solely to disappointment in love, but to the conflict of a mind ill at ease with itself respecting religion? What if she were at this moment wavering between her desire to embrace the Catholic faith and the fear of offending her father?"

"You amaze me," said Father Stirling. "Can this be so?"

"I have it on good authority, and as it is not under the seal of confession, I may tell you how I know it. Miss Winover, a young lady, who is—as you are perhaps aware—a very good Catholic, has lately made the acquaintance of Miss Singleton, and has considered it her duty to tell me the blessed change, which has been gradually operating in her friend's sentiments on the vital subject of religion. Miss Singleton has actually resided for a year in one of those Protestant Sisterhoods which are now becoming common. Such is the high compliment the heretics pay us that, even while refusing to believe our religion, they try to copy it—in a very bungling manner, to be sure. Miss Winover described this Religious House! I was uncharitable enough to laugh heartily at the picture. But it is so droll to see Protestants playing at Catholics. The house is under the direction of Dr. Formula, that half-way house between the Anglican and Catholic Church. Archbishop Middleton wonders, and some zealous Catholics complain that he does not come over to us. For my part, *entre nous*, I am satisfied he does us more real service by remaining where he is. He brings a good many converts to Rome, if he does not come himself. But pardon this digression. Naturally enough, Miss Singleton, having discovered the errors of Protestantism, is not satisfied to halt between two opinions, and is tired of sitting at the feet of Dr. Formula. She wishes to belong to us, and indeed she is only deterred by the dread of her father's displeasure."

"How strange is all this," said Father Stirling. "Madeline Singleton wishes to become a Catholic! It is not so much her father's anger she dreads: it is the fear of rendering him unhappy. She is his only child. What would become of him were she to turn apostate."

"Apostate!" repeated Father Wiley, with startling emphasis. "Is it Clement Stirling who speaks?"

It was quite evident that Father Stirling had been thinking aloud. He replied, quickly:—

"I speak but as the world speaks. You know I was called an apostate when I recanted vows which had been made for me when a child. Her father would curse her as an apostate. I know the old man well; he is inflexible."

"And do you put his anger, his bigoted rage, or his peace of mind in competition with the salvation of a human soul," retorted Father Wiley, with a greater degree of unction than his quiet, self-possessed manner usually displayed. "Must I remind you of the important dogma of the Faith?—'Without the pale of the Church there is no salvation.'"*

Father Stirling felt a sudden contraction of the heart at these words, which reminded him so forcibly that he was no longer a free agent, but had become a mere instrument of the mightiest spiritual despotism ever planned by man. He flushed and grew pale by turns,

* "*Hanc veram Catholicam fidem, extra quam nemo salvus esse potest.*"—This true Catholic Faith, out of which no one can be saved. —*Bull of Pope Pius IV., touching the form of the oath of the Profession of Faith.*

"This is the Catholic Faith, which except a man believe faithfully, he cannot be saved."—*The Creed of St. Anthanasius, accepted by the Anglican Church.*

as he said, in a constrained and unnatural voice—

"You think then, that I should assist in leading Miss Singleton back to the true fold?"

"Most undoubtedly, I think so," replied Father Wiley; "but I do not offer my opinion officiously. The question especially concerns yourself, and I know no one better qualified than yourself to arrive at a proper decision."

CHAPTER III.

ECCLESIASTICAL CELIBACY VERSUS MARRIAGE.

After the compliment dexterously conveyed in his last words, Father Wiley gradually turned the conversation into other channels, for he perceived that Father Stirling had no wish to prolong the subject. These men frequently discussed doctrinal points, and the principal distinctions between the Romish and Reformed Faiths and Church Government, in an amicable and familiar manner, and with a latitude which would appear strange to a layman, who judges of the clergy solely as they appear in a professional point of view. On the present occasion they glided into the question of the celibacy of the clergy, a subject suggested by what Father Stirling had confessed as to his own recent feelings in society. Father Stirling defended the practice of the Protestants and the Greek Church in permitting ecclesiastics to marry. Father Wiley advocated the practice of the Church of Rome, and spoke, as follows—

"What is it you complain of in our celibacy? That it does not work well in practice. I shall not dwell on the beautiful, the sublime theory on which it rests, in common with all the infallible decisions of the Catholic Church; that a priest, a man who is found worthy to serve in the sacred mysteries of the faith, and minister in the solemn sacrifice of the Mass, should be a holy man—should be capable of subduing that which is most debasing and animal in our nature. Neither is it necessary to point out to you the singular advantage gained in intellectual power and spiritual strength by this moral restraint. The first duty of an acolyte in the ancient secret societies (the true supporters of learning in their time), was to subdue the animal within him. It was the same with the institution of chivalry. Chastity was enforced on a candidate for the honour of knighthood. Let us leave all these beautiful theories, and look at the question practically, like men who have had experience of the world. To take then a lower, more prosaic view of the matter, such as we are compelled sooner or later to take of most sublunary things. Is it such a hardship to remain unmarried? How many laymen remain old bachelors from choice! Are we not spared the trouble, the expense, the daily care and worry, the countless anxieties and responsibilities which weigh down the married man and father of a family? Are we not secure from being made the victims of the blandishments, trickeries, wiles, inconstancy, caprice, deceit, and falsehood of women? But, from a strictly professional point of view—how can a man do his duty as a priest, and at the same time bring up a family? How find time for preaching, studying, visiting the sick, burying the dead, marrying the living, christening, confessing, and all the varied multiplicity of parochial duties—and in addition rear a large family? My question receives a practical answer when we observe the lives led by the celibate and married clergy. Where do you find among the clergy of the Anglican Church, or Protestants generally, that simplicity of life, that single-hearted devotion and concentration of all the energies of the soul to professional duties—to the cause of God and the Church, which characterize, with such few exceptions, the clergy of the Romish Church? Compare the *curé* in France, or the village priest in Ireland, or England, who weds the Church, and gives his whole thoughts to his pastoral duties, with the Protestant clergy, busied with their families, anxious about the morrow, jostling each other in the hunt after clerical prizes. How can it be otherwise? An Anglican curate falls in love and marries, say at twenty-one. He is fortunate if he gets a living worth eighty or a hundred a year; and at forty he may have ten children. That is to say, ten children may have been born to him; but how is he to feed, clothe, and keep them alive? Education seems to be out of the question. That is the reason why, although the Anglican is the most richly endowed Church Establishment in the world—two-thirds or three-fourths of her clergy are always poor, dissatisfied, and envious of the dignitaries and hierarchy. Even the Bishops, who are so much better paid than ours, cannot be rich, for they spend their wealth on their families and relatives. The Protestant clergy must be selfish, rapacious, ambitious, greedy after the loaves and fishes, for they cannot see their own flesh and blood starve. Naturally they love their own children more than the poor. No sooner does an ecclesiastic achieve distinction in the Anglican Church, than he is surrounded by a host of relatives and connexions, to provide for. Hence the flagrant cases of nepotism which are continually charged against the bishops and the dignitaries—the traffic in benefices, &c., which is carried on as a matter of course, and of which no one is ashamed.

"Another consequence of the system is that the Protestant clergy are cowards when compared with the Catholic clergy, and never risk their lives so fearlessly as the latter.* The reason is obvious. The Protestant clergy are married; the family again! They have more to live for, and consequently are fonder of life. A crowning illustration of this, and the inconvenience of marriage to the priest, is to be found in the missionary life. The sums which are expended by the

* The reader must remember that it is a Romish priest who speaks. The author, however, would observe that, without wishing to introduce any invidious comparisons, the courage of the Catholic clergy is unquesable, and does not in his humble opinion always meet with due appreciation from Protestants. Out of numerous instances which might be adduced, he will only refer to one well-known: the death of the Archbishop of Paris, at the barricades in 1848, when he went forth to check the fray, and was heard frequently to repeat to himself the words—"*Bonus autem pastor dat vitam suam pro ovibus suis.*" A more noble death man never died! His name will be embalmed in history along with that of the monk Almachius or Telemachus, who lost his life by rushing into the Flavian Ampitheatre, and endeavouring to separate the combatants, an act which caused the gladiatorial shows to be abolished. Tradition has preserved the memory of this intrepid action, and we have got something approaching to the hero's name. Had he been a destroyer instead of a preserver of human life, how many volumes would have been written in his praise!

Protestants in sending out missionaries and their families are enormous. And what have they to show for it? For a tithe of the sum our missions do a great deal more work. That is one of the principal reasons why, under God's providence, Rome is Christianizing the whole world, and evincing her claim to the title of the *Catholic* Church, while the Anglican Church is simply the Church of England, and nothing more. Nothing more, do I say? She is not even *that!* she is neither the Church of Ireland, nor of Scotland. In England she is only the Church of the upper and wealthy middle-classes. She is not the Church of the poor, and the various dissenting sects probably average one half of the actual worshippers. Our missionaries go forth into every land untrameled by the ties of kith and kin. The Protestant missionary drives a bargain for the support of his wife and family before he sets forth to the scene of his labours. Consequently, where Protestantism can send one, Rome can send ten! And then, as to the effect on those to be converted, by the example of a Catholic missionary priest, whose whole life is a sacrifice, and a Protestant missionary who makes as little sacrifice as possible, and lives comfortably, with his wife and family about him, I need not enlarge. Results speak for themselves!

"Such, my dear Father Stirling, are some of the beneficial results from the admirable principle of celibacy in our church. Catholicism is advancing both at home and abroad in the most triumphant manner. The Anglican Church from the inherent weakness in her system cannot convert on a grand scale. She is not succeeding in India, where she possesses unlimited political sway, and which is her most flourishing colony. Here in England, the Establishment is distracted by intestinal divisions. Everything foretells the commencement of the end. Heresy has seen its palmiest days, and is now crumbling to decay. It may not be in our time, but most assuredly before many, many years—Rome will receive her most prodigal child into her communion."

As these views may be considered even too visionary for a Jesuit priest, I will insert here an extract from Mr. Smith's admirable work, "Thorndale, or the Conflict of Opinions." The following graphic passage is put into the mouth of Seckendorf, a German Rationalist:—

"Is it one among the symptoms of intellectual progress that there is a movement in England towards the Roman Catholic Church? Is this movement at all connected with some political movement, some monarchical tendency? Does it result from pure love of truth and the spirit of inquiry? I, who was brought up in the great Catholic church, have my partialities towards her, and might not be the fittest judge. How do you read this matter? To me it seems not improbable that that ragged urchin who is chalking up 'No Popery' on the walls of London, may live to see High Mass performed in St. Paul's Cathedral. He, himself, will be kneeling, an old man, bare-headed, on the pavement, to be sprinkled by the holy water as priests pass by in gorgeous procession, bearing the immaculate Virgin on their shoulders. Half your clergy, half your aristocracy, and every idle woman are already ours. All who love pomp and sentiment better than perplexing dogmas will welcome the change. As to the mob, we know of old how they are to be converted. The good Moslems knew and practised the art long ago. Not always is the sword necessary. The Muezzin ascends the tower and calls to prayer; the people pelt him with stones; he ascends again and calls still louder and the people throw fewer stones; he still ascends, still calls, and the people drop their stones from their hands and fall upon their knees. There is but one body in England from whom a stout resistance may be expected. The Dissenters will not convert. The descendants of the old Puritans—the Republicans in religion will stand out to the last. They will not convert, but they will *burn;* they are combustible. And if an age too fastidious rejects the aid of fire, even in so great an emergency, there are your colonies—they can be transported. England purified from their presence will again be embraced in the One Holy Catholic and Apostolic Church."

"But come," said Father Wiley, relapsing into his more familiar or almost jocular manner of speaking. "It is now your turn, my dear Stirling. Put yourself in the position of a heretic and a Protestant clergyman, and defend the marriage of ecclesiastics. You want to marry. Come, begin."

Again Father Stirling could not resist scanning the speaker's countenance. But Father Wiley bore the scrutiny as though he had spoken in perfect sincerity, with no consciousness of conveying a double meaning. Father Stirling endeavoured to clothe his thoughts in the same amicable familiar phraseology, although it was evident that his reply betrayed a strong personal feeling.

"My dear Wiley, we are agreed as to the sublime idea on which is founded the ordinance of celibacy in our church; but practically I cannot agree with you that it works so well. I cannot sympathise with your depreciating tone in speaking of women. Were you not so stoically independent in your own strength, you would be willing to admit, the society of women is beneficial and salutary to all men. I do not enter into the question of the passions, but I refer more particularly to the moral and intellectual refining influence which woman exerts over the soul of man. You, speaking of them but by report, dwell upon the tricks, deceit, and inconstancy of the sex. You are silent as to the courage, the disinterestedness, the tenderness, the sympathy—in short the love of women. Ask the married men how they regard the dull, cheerless life of celibacy. Oh! believe me, you thoroughly fail to comprehend love and marriage, if you think these words signify only brief delirious joys akin to guilty pleasures. What the united sense of mankind in all ages has seen in honourable love—in marriage, is the sweet and serene consciousness of knowing that you have one tried heart to lean on amid the storms and adversities of life. Admit there is something deeply interesting and pathetic in a man and woman uniting in youth that they may assist each other to bear the crosses and miseries of life. And then the crown of marriage is the experience of the parental feelings. Who can watch a mother playing with her infant, or a father forgetting all the hard rubs of the world in the bosom of his domestic circle, with his children climbing upon his knees, and not perceive a touching illustration of the Divine principle of love? Oh, Wiley, I doubt if the man who has not known these tender ties, not felt the overflowing emotions—the sentiment of universal brotherhood which they engender, can really possess that full and perfect development of the heart which is absolutely necessary to the due discharge of the priestly office. We are called fathers, yet we are forbidden to know a father's feelings, as alone they can be known by actual individual experience. This is the way in which the good Protestant clergy look at the question, and I am disposed to think they are right. Remember also that the Greek Church permits its clergy to marry."

Father Stirling stopped rather abruptly as though conscious that he had spoken somewhat too frankly.

"Upon my word, Stirling, you are half a heretic," said Wiley jocularly. "I must keep my eye upon you or you will be recanting some day, as Cranmer did. It is true," he added, "we are debarred from those tender ties of which you speak so feelingly, but we may avail ourselves of the refinement of female society. I confess I should miss the neatness and order which my niece has established here. I have the consolation of knowing that I minister to my own comfort and do a charitable action at the same time in offering a home to Miss Pyne."

At this moment there was a low knock at the folding doors which separated the dining from the drawing room, and Miss Pyne obeyed Father Wiley's summons to enter. She was a young woman about twenty-five, with dark hair and the pale complexion of one who did not take sufficient out-door exercise. Her features were comely and her figure good. But her personal advantages were marred by the extreme nervousness and embarrassment, which were painfully apparent in every look and gesture. She kept her eyes fixed on the ground, and did not raise them when spoken to by Father Stirling, whose kindly greeting she acknowledged with a low reverence.

"I thought," she said, in a very faint and hesitating voice, "that you might be ready for tea."

"That we are, Selina," said Father Wiley, who seemed in unusually good spirits, "and after tea you shall favour us with some music. Father Stirling has never heard you sing. Your Reverence has no idea what a sweet voice Selina has."

Miss Pyne sat down before the urn which a female servant brought in, and made the tea, but in spite of Father Wiley's amiability and attempts to make the conversation general, she answered briefly, chiefly in monosyllables, and when not spoken to remained silent. From time to time she cast furtive glances at Father Wiley as if she stood in awe of him. Father Stirling wondered whether she feared the Jesuit? whether he was in private, stern and inflexible, and made her feel that she ate the bread of dependence? It never suggested itself to the unsuspicious mind of Father Stirling that there might be other and darker reasons for Miss Pyne's want of self-possession. Innocent himself, he had none of that uncharitableness which is the characteristic of the sinner, and when persons hinted at the somewhat questionable position occupied by the Jesuit's niece! Father Stirling honestly and conscientiously disbelieved the inuendo thus meant to be conveyed.

After tea Miss Pyne was prevailed upon to sit down to the piano and sing one of those touching Scotch melodies, which though now old-fashioned in the opinion of young ladies, who prefer screaming Verdi, or "Hoop-de-dooden-do," and other nigger melodies and popular songs of the day—sad rubbish as many of them are—will ever remain favourites with those who like good music wedded to real poetry. The song which Miss Pyne sang was that deeply affecting ballad "Auld Robin Grey." The words of the original song are by Lady Anne Barnard. It is a pity that it has shared the fate of many favourite songs, and has had a sequel added to it, written in the worst possible taste. The singer faltered, and made two or three abortive attempts.

"How ridiculous, Selina," exclaimed Father Wiley, in a sharp tone of displeasure, "you know you can sing beautifully when you choose; and to-night, when I expressly desired his Reverence to hear my favourite air—"

"Nay—nay, you are too harsh," said Father Stirling, and turning to the performer, he made a few kind and encouraging remarks, which appeared to put her much more at ease, for she succeeded in getting through all but the last verse, when her voice, which was clear, sweet, and tolerably powerful, abruptly broke down.

Father Stirling was deeply affected, not only at the plaintive music and words, but because there was a real or fancied resemblance between the singer's voice and that of Miss Singleton. He had averted his head to hide his emotion, and remained silent for about a minute after the notes ceased. When he turned to thank Miss Pyne, her place was vacant; she had abruptly left the room.

CHAPTER IV.

JESUIT SCHEMES.

No sooner had his guest departed at ten o'clock than Father Wiley withdrew to his private cabinet. This was a small oak-panelled room, containing an escritoire, a few high-backed grotesquely carved chairs, such as were in use about a century ago, and a well-filled book-case. There was also a little iron door, which opened into a fire-proof safe built into the wall. The only ornament which the room possessed was an oil painting, a fine original portrait of Ignatius Loyola, holding in his hand that remarkable work the "Spiritual Exercises."

But the room was not untenanted. I demand pardon of its occupant for the apparent slight conveyed in describing the room and its accessories first. Let me now introduce the reader to Father Monaghan, Romish priest and learned Jesuit, distinguished member of the *professi*—that is, those who have taken the four vows, Chastity, Poverty, Obedience, and to travel everywhere in the service of the Pope—recently sent from Rome to occupy, near the person of Father Wiley, the post of *socius*. Before proceeding further to describe the worthy *socius*, it will be necessary to give the reader some insight into the views of Father Wiley with reference to Father Stirling.

As the reader has perhaps already inferred, the Jesuit's design was to make his friend a member of the society of Jesus. To this he was impelled by two strong inducements—first, his own personal wish; second, but infinitely stronger, his allegiance to the order, whose commands left him no option. Say what we will, every man or woman is naturally a propagandist. We all desire to convert—to bring everybody else round to our own way of thinking, either for their own temporal or eternal welfare. Father Wiley wished to see his friend become a member of the order of which he (Father Wiley) was such a zealous supporter. This had been the Jesuit's ultimate object from the time when he first began to acquire an influence over his young pupil, who had now achieved such a brilliant reputation as a preacher, and what was better, was so generally esteemed as an earnest priest and good man. Father Wiley looked upon Clement Stirling as, in a great degree, his own creation. He was proud of his work, and let us do him the justice to say, he was not actuated solely by motives of personal interest; he fully believed his friend qualified to adorn the order of Loyola, and to find therein a more ample scope for his great abilities than he at present possessed, provided the pulse of earthly ambition could once be awakened within his heart. He had several times indirectly intimated his wish to Clement. He had never yet formally proposed to him to become a Jesuit, for reasons which will shortly appear.

As I am drawing no mere monster of motiveless malignity, I am desirous of showing all the extenuating causes of Father Wiley's conduct, however reprehensible and disastrous in its consequences. He was a sheer passive instrument under the orders of his immediate superior, the head of the order in England. This was a man advanced in age who took but little active part in affairs, and *he* was in his turn of course subject to the orders issued by the authority of the Father General, the supreme head of the Jesuits at Rome. Father Wiley's periodical reports had given ample details on the subject of Father Stirling. The great abilities of the latter, his fame as a preacher, his general reputation for piety, austerity, and above all, *zeal*, had marked him out as too important an acquisition to the order to be suffered to escape. To whet Father Wiley's desire to bring this important convert into the ranks of the society, it had been signified to him that on Clement Stirling becoming a member, Father Wiley would be appointed General of the Jesuits in England. Thus was the Rev. Father stimulated by his vow of obedience, his personal ambition, in addition to his own private wishes, to see Clement Stirling bound to him by the still closer ties of the fraternity of Loyola. Father Wiley firmly believed in the complete restoration of the Jesuits to their pristine power. As the wish is often father to the thought, this man, in other respects a clear-sighted man of he world, was quite in earnest in what he had said to Father Stirling relative to the approaching triumph of the Papacy. Thus he read the ecclesiastical signs of the times. In the divisions among Protestants he did not see the strength of zeal, but weakness. In the intestinal feuds in the Establishment, in the conversions to, and evident leaning towards, Popery, fomented by the order of which he was the practical and virtual leader in England, in the attitudes of the High Church and Tractarian parties, the increase of dissent, and above all Catholic Emancipation, he saw what he believed to be decided and unmistakeable symptoms of the decline of the "Great Protestant Heresy." He believed that Rome would again in the nineteenth century owe her triumph to the same institution which had contributed so materially to defend her in the sixteenth! His grand ambition was to restore the palmy days of the society. With this, of course, a considerable share of personal ambition was mingled.

Two grand obstacles to the fulfilment of his day-dream the Jesuit did not perceive or appreciate. The first is the entire change which has taken place in the constitution of society and public opinion. The spread of scientific knowledge and moral enlightenment has materially altered the conditions which rendered the Jesuit Institute practicable or necessary. Men are now extremely jealous of liberty, so that the enormous power which the Society of Jesus wielded in the sixteenth and seventeenth centuries has become a chimera in the nineteenth century. There is no wish to impugn here the sincerity of intention which actuated, nor the real good achieved, by the Jesuits. But, like the knight-templars and many other medieval institutions, their day and generation has passed away. It would be a question for a casuist to determine whether the benefit which their zeal conferred, was not counterbalanced by their attempts—in many instances but too successful—to check the progress of independent thought and human liberty.

They certainly excelled in the art of taming men, and they acted in general from a desire to subjugate man for his own good. There can be no doubt that the leading idea pervading the Jesuits was to subject the whole world to the spiritual dominion of the Pope, under the conscientious conviction that this spiritual allegiance would be to the benefit of the lieges. It is impossible, I imagine, for any intelligent reader to trace the career of the Jesuits, without being struck with the sublime self-sacrifice of the individual will, which enabled this extraordinary fraternity to extend itself, in so short a time, not over Europe merely, but into Asia and South America, till at length it owed its dissolution to the supreme head of that religion, which saw in its former principal support a dangerous rival in power. In the outcry against this grand scheme of mental and moral conquest, people seem to forget that every religion aims at the same object, to conquer the human will. Guizot, in his history of civilization, writes thus:—

"What does every religion lay claim to? The government of human passions, and of human will. Every religion is a curb, a power, a government. It comes in the name of divine law to subdue human nature. Therefore human liberty is its especial antagonist, which it is its object to vanquish.

To this purpose is its mission, its hope directed."

But what if Papal Rome had succeeded in her unparalleled ambition? She aimed at a despotism far greater than that exercised by Imperial Rome, to place not a temporal, but a spiritual yoke on the whole world. A temporal yoke may be borne—a spiritual tyranny never can. Papal Rome then actually aspired to do what the Rome of the Cæsars never ventured to attempt. That she succeeded to such an extent is a proof of the low ebb to which arts, letters, and civilization had fallen in the middle and justly-termed dark ages. The Rome of Tiberius, Nero, Caligula, and Domitian did not dictate the religion of Jupiter. They left every nation, even the Jews, perfect religious liberty. The nation which could produce a Virgil, a Horace, a Juvenal, a Tacitus, a Livy, a Pliny, was too wise, too enlightened, to try to force one creed upon the whole world. It seems never to have been intended that all men should worship at the same altars, and with the same rites, and the attempt of any one religion to force itself upon the whole human race never can be successful. Where it does partially succeed, or seem to succeed, it makes a hundred slaves, a hundred hypocrites, for one conscientious convert. The gigantic ambition of the Papal church, at the height of its power, makes one shudder for the prospects of humanity. To make us all think exactly alike on religion, a subject on which no two human minds can think exactly alike; to force the civilized European, the Japanese, the South American, the African Hottentot, all to repeat the same creed, all to adopt the same worship, to have the same sacrifice of the mass offered by priests all over the world, under the tropics, and in the Polar regions; in Vienna, London, Paris, Edinburgh; in Pekin, Timbuctoo, Australia, and the Sandwich Islands; and to have in Rome the centre of this religion embracing the globe. Well might the popes use the form, "*Urbit et Orbi!*" This grand project of spiritual conquest, sublime in its very audacity, is what Papal Rome dreamt, planned, concocted in the middle ages. This is what Papal Rome dreams, plans, and concocts, now in the nineteenth century. No wonder that she failed; no wonder that the reformation burst forth. To realize such an extraordinary idea men must cease to be free-agents, reasoning, thinking beings, and become automata, puppets, machines.

The second grand obstacle to the fulfilment of Father Wiley's day-dream, another reason that the Jesuits will never exert the influence once wielded by them, is, that independently of the great change in public opinion, it would require another man of Loyola's genius and enthusiastic temperament to attempt the restoration of what he created. Jesuitism soon became tainted with the worldly spirit, and departed from the objects of its austere founder. Speaking of the order in the middle of the seventeenth century, Ranke says:— "The Jesuits were incapable of any longer preserving the influence with which at an earlier period they had governed men's minds. In fact, however, they no longer had a mind to subject the world to themselves, and to imbue it with a religious spirit; much rather had their own spirit fallen under the influence of the world; their only endeavour was to render themselves indispensable to mankind, in whatever way they could succeed in doing so." Moreover, its internal government, the system of mutual espionage, the slavish obedience, and perfect annihilation of the will is not favourable to the growth of individual intellectual development. The society has never produced a man who could be compared to its founder. Nor are its principles calculated to produce men of independent minds.

In accordance with the traditional policy of the society, it was not enough to spur Father Wiley on to the desired end by the strong impulse of personal ambition. He was closely watched, lest, yielding to a feeling of human weakness, he might hesitate to coerce his friend. The Rev. Father was well aware of this. He was also occasionally quickened by intimations that if he did not succeed within a certain period, his dilatory proceedings would be construed into a want of zeal, if not a breach of his vow of implicit unconditional obedience,* and he would be superseded by a more effective and unscrupulous agent. It was under this moral—or immoral—pressure that Father Wiley had in his report, some time previously, written as follows:—

"The conversion of Father Stirling must be a work of time. Every thought in his

* An attentive observation of the laws that were successively given to this society, shows that one of the chief objects by which they were dictated. was that all the common ties which bind men together should be completely cut asunder. Love of kindred was condemned as a carnal affection. Whoever renounced his property for the sake of entering into the society, was not to relinquish it to his relati ns, but to mete it out to the poor. Whoever once entered neither received nor despatched letters without their being first read by a superior. The society will have nothing less than the whole man; it seeks to lay fetters on all his inclinations. * * * For in this society obedience takes the place of every other tie, and every other motive, that the world can present to human activity; obedience for its own sake, and without respect to the end to which it is directed.—*Ranke's Popes of Rome.*

heart is known to me, both through the medium of the confessional and the terms of intimacy on which we live. Indeed the Rev. Father is so singularly guileless that the agents whom I employ bring me no intelligence which I have not already learned from his own lips. Such however is the Rev. Father's independence of mind, such his jealousy of any interference with his liberty, that I know he frets under the spiritual bonds he already wears, and that he would startle at the idea of that strict discipline and implicit obedience which characterise the order of the blessed Loyola. This is the true cause why I have never yet ventured to do more than insinuate my opinion of his fitness for the Company of Jesus, fearing lest a more open course might sow the seeds of mistrust and dissension between us, and so lose the influence I now have over him."

On another occasion Father Wiley wrote as follows :—

"After long deliberation I have come to

the conclusion that there is one way, and only one, by which this most able and eloquent man may be made ours. His life is at present spotless. If he could only be detected in one little deviation from the path of virtue, some slight infraction of his religious vows, one little venial sin—such is his strong feeling of conscientiousness, that I should from that moment become entirely his master, and could dictate my own terms. Recent discoveries of the Rev. Father's state of mind lead me to believe that this is practicable; and thus a temptation of a certain kind, skilfully applied, followed by a deviation from the strict path of rectitude, would undoubtedly be the means of obtaining a most useful and zealous agent to the society, and secure to the Rev. Father himself, a field for the due exercise of his great abilities, and would minister to his temporal happiness and eternal glory. Thus out of a small modicum of evil would spring an incalculable amount of good, and the Rev. Father would illustrate the important principle of Molinos:—'If the inferior part be without sin, the superior part grows proud, and pride is the greatest sin. Consequently the flesh ought to sin, in order that the soul may remain humble; sin producing humility, becomes a ladder to ascend to heaven.' I do not venture to reduce this principle to practice without an express permission from the supreme authority. I am but an humble instrument in the hands of my superiors. I await orders in accordance with this grand law of our constitutions: '*Et sibi quisque persuadeat, quod qui sub obedientia vivunt, se ferri ac regi a divina providentia per superiores suos sinere debent, perinde ac cadaver essent.*'" *

Father Wiley's report was carefully analyzed, and the abominable hint which it conveyed thoroughly understood and acted upon in the reply which he received from Rome. He was not told in so many words to

* "And let each be persuaded that they who live under obedience ought to allow themselves to be borne about and governed by the divine providence, acting in their superiors just as if they were a corpse."—RANKE.

entice his friend to sin in order to entrap his conscience and govern him through his fears; but he was reminded in the most emphatic language that Father Stirling must become a member of the company of Jesus, which would be doubly benefited by the *prestige* conferred by the conversion of so celebrated a personage acting as an example, and by the direct advantages of his zeal and abilities; that so highly an important and laudable an object sanctified the means employed; and in order to remove any possible scruples of conscience which Father Wiley might still retain, he received as *socius* the Father Monaghan already introduced to the reader.

CHAPTER V.

FATHER MONAGHAN.

FATHER MONAGHAN had been educated at Rome, and had lived there long enough to outgrow any special veneration for his country. England he had always hated, and his long residence in "The Eternal City" had so completely naturalized or denaturalized him, and banished from his memory early *souvenirs* of the Emerald Isle, that he was now at fifty, a temporal as well as a spiritual subject of the Pope. All ties, all feelings had been swallowed up in his religious calling. He was most emphatically a Romish priest. He was deeply read in the works of the most subtle casuists of the order—such as Escobar, Mariana, Sanchez, Bauny, Busembaum, and others. If Father Wiley doubted which of two courses to follow, he was to consult the *socius* and be guided implicitly by the latter's directions. Thus the younger Jesuit delivered his conscience into the keeping of the elder, and saw himself converted into an intellectually powerful, and (as he believed) a morally irresponsible agent in proselytizing his friend.

Wiley knew that the *socius* was acting as a spy upon, as well as an adviser to him, and although (knowing his own value and firmly believing there was no other man capable of stepping into his shoes and bringing to a satisfactory issue all the machinations of which he held the clew) he thought little of the implied threat to supersede him, he still felt the necessity of bringing the affair of Father Stirling to a prompt conclusion. It must be confessed that Father Wiley might, without laying himself open to the charge of vanity, laugh in his sleeve at the bare idea of being supplanted by his *socius!*

Imagine a man below the middle height, and remarkably obese, with a round, bullet-shaped head, covered with closely-cropped hair, of a whitey brown hue, caused by the sprinkling of the original red colour with grey; a low forehead, little ferret eyes, and coarse features scarred with the small pox. Add to this a suit of rusty black, buttoned closely up, displaying not the slightest vestige of linen anywhere, and thickly powdered with snuff, which the *socius* took in profusion from a common round wooden box; and a general and offensive slovenliness. Such was the appearance presented by Father Monaghan—a striking contrast to the handsome, elegant, and scrupulously neat Father Wiley. I have said that all ties and associations had been swallowed up in Father Monaghan's calling. One exception must be made. The *socius* was very fond of the national beverage of his country—whiskey—and habit had enabled him to indulge in it almost with impunity. A bottle and glass stood on the table, and the Rev. Father occasionally helped himself as if mechanically, while engaged in marking, collating, and transcribing passages from sundry volumes. One must not judge by externals, and although the hands and face of Father Monaghan did not look as if they had made a recent acquaintance with soap and water, it would be wrong to infer therefrom that he was not morally pure. If so, he did not illustrate the text "Cleanliness is next to godliness;" and those who came very close to him could testify that the odour of his sanctity was no mere metaphorical expression. Father Wiley never took the hand of his *socius* if he could help doing so, and in spite of his courtly, self-possessed manner, found it difficult at times to repress the manifestation of disgust. It would seem indeed as if the annoyance of having Father Monaghan as his guest, and being compelled to associate with him daily, was intended as an effective penance to urge Father Wiley to decisive action. Father

Monaghan perceived the aversion which he inspired, and took a malicious pleasure (especially when excited with whiskey) in making his authority felt.

"Well," he said, speaking in a peculiar accent, a compound of the Irish and Italian, "you have had a long afternoon with him. Has anything been settled yet?"

"Not yet, your Reverence," said Father Wiley, submissively.

"Humph!" said the *socius*, taking a pinch of snuff. "I hope there are no private feelings at the bottom of all this delay."

Father Wiley replied—

"I have undertaken to bring Father Stirling into the order. I am pledged, and am doing my best to keep my word, but as I have already said, this is a very delicate case, which requires time. Father Stirling is very different from those Anglican curates whom I catch like sparrows. What will succeed with them and other ordinary men will not do with him. I have however thought of a plan which I feel quite confident will succeed, but—"

"More scruples of conscience, I suppose," interrupted the *socius*. "Father Stirling is your friend, but, by a rule of our society, the love of kindred is condemned as a carnal affection. What, then, ought mere friendship to be?"

"Your Reverence little knows me," replied Father Wiley, "if you imagine that I would hesitate an instant to sacrifice all personal feelings to the advancement of the order. It is not because Father Stirling is my friend, but because he is little short of a saint, and I see no possible means of inducing him to become a member of the company, save by tempting him to commit a sin. If you knew Father Stirling's reputation for piety, you would not wonder at these scruples."

"Have you consulted your Liguori?" said Father Monaghan.

"I have," replied Father Wiley, "and I only desire the opinion of your Reverence as to whether the cases he cites apply to the present difficulty. But I see your Reverence has been taking some notes, doubtless, bearing on this very question?"

"Well," replied the *socius*, mollified by Father Wiley's courteous speech, "your case of conscience seems to me ample and in every respect provided for in Liguori. And first of all, as to the authority of this admirable man, to whom Clement XIII. said when compelling him to assume the Episcopal dignity, which, through humility, he was unwilling to accept, 'I am content that you should govern your diocese within your own doors; sufficient for me is your very shadow to govern and improve your diocese.' To whom Clement XIV. said, when Liguori desired to resign his office, 'I am content that you should govern the church from your bed; one prayer of yours, to God, even from your bed, will more avail your flock than a thousand visits from another.'" The *socius* continued to multiply testimonies to the value of Liguori's teaching, which it is unnecessary to relate. He added that the church of Rome had unanimously declared his works to contain not one word worthy of censure, and expressed full and final approval by canonizing the author in the year 1839.

And what was the teaching of this canonized author whose works contain *not one word worthy of censure?* that it is lawful to induce any one to commit a lesser evil for the avoiding of a greater one. "Thus you may be able to persuade any one who is determined to commit murder, that he should only cut off the hand, however, of the same person, not another chosen person."* How applicable was this precious precept to Father Wiley's designs against Stirling. The latter was evidently wavering in his faith. He had just impugned in argument the institution of celibacy. He had begun to doubt on some grave dogmas. What was one venial sin, compared with the terrible sin of heresy, of

* Moral Theology of Liguori; p. 419.

falling away from the faith ? and this sin would be the means of establishing Father Stirling more firmly than ever under the authority of the church. Another of the saint's teachings is "That it is lawful, not only not to take away, but even to afford occasion to sin, if, by doing so, a good result will be accomplished. To co-operate only materially in supplying only the matter and power of sinning, or by exhibiting an object, is lawful, if the following conditions are present: 1st—If there be a need of such co-operation, or if the co-operation be of itself good, or, at least, indifferent. 2nd—If it be done with a good intention, and for, good cause, and not that you may assist another in sin."

Such was the kind of teaching which the *socius* accumulated. How could Father Wiley retain any scruples in the face of the Jesuit doctrine of Probability, enunciated by Busembaum, that in doubtful cases a man may venture to follow an opinion, of the soundness of which he is not himself convinced, provided, beforehand, that it be defended by some respectable author. Father Wiley believed that Clement Stirling might be conquered by the skilful direction of his passions, and determined to lose no time in etting loose upon his friend all the powerful machinery of the confessional. He likewise communicated to Father Monaghan that in all probability a wealthy heiress, moving in fashionable circles, would soon become a convert to Rome, and perhaps the inmate of a Jesuit convent, in which case her wealth would belong to the order.

The *socius* was so much pleased with this intelligence, that he insisted upon Father Wiley accompanying him in a glass of whiskey. Father Wiley, who had an exquisite taste in wine, drank the spirit with a very ill grace, much to the gratification of Father Monaghan, who was now passing into the malicious stage in his cups, and could not resist saying in conclusion:

"I am very glad that your Reverence has

determined to act at last, for I should have been extremely sorry to have been obliged to interfere personally, or take the matter out of your hands."

Father Wiley was in such a rage that he did not trust himself to speak. He watched the retreating figure of Father Monaghan, with an extremely unsteady gait rolling off to bed, and then relieved his feelings by a strong Saxon exclamation. Finally, he could not help laughing, so irresistibly droll seeemed the idea of the snuffy, slovenly, "swipy" Father Monaghan, occupying his (Father Wiley's) place in society.

Let us now return to the unsuspicious object of these Machiavelian machinations.

CHAPTER VI.

A FEMALE PROPAGANDIST.

For two days after the evening spent at Mr. Wiley's house, Father Stirling continually debated with himself how he should act in reference to Miss Singleton. He was inspired by a strong curiosity to learn of his own knowledge whether a change had really taken place in her religious ideas; and if such were the case, what line of conduct was thereby imposed on him. Each had been the involuntary instrument of wrecking the other's hopes of temporal happiness. There was then the more reason why each should assist the other to gain happiness eternal. If the theory held by some, that *every* human event is fashioned by superhuman means, were true, might it not lie within the inscrutable designs of Providence that thus he was to be made the instrument of salvation to her?

Clement Stirling knelt and prayed. He asked the counsel of Heaven in this dilemma. But, alas! his prayers were not answered; no Divine inspiration taught him what steps he should take.

"No, no," he exclaimed, "I am no longer worthy to pray; my soul is sullied with the pleasures of the world."

He could come to no decision as to the proper course of action, so peculiar was his situation with regard to Miss Singleton. How could he with any propriety propose an interview with her, even if the high-spirited Colonel would hear of such a thing? Thus the matter looked to the man-of-the-world. But, on the other hand, to the priest, how criminal seemed his inaction, while this wandering lamb was perhaps seeking celestial food, hungering for the manna of truth, thirsting for the fountain of living water.

Thus Clement Stirling tortured himself, striving in vain to analyze and discriminate his motives; how far he was actuated by the earthly passion of a lover, how far by the zeal of a Christian teacher? It was, indeed, a question to puzzle a causist. If the former feelings predominated, it was criminal in him to see Madeline. If the latter, it was criminal in him not to seek an interview. But as he could not rest without gaining some tidings of Miss Singleton, he at length on the third day after his interview with Wiley, called upon Miss Winover.

This lady has been already introduced to the reader. She was one of the ladies whose colloquy Father Stirling over-heard on the night of the ball. Father Stirling had a slight acquaintance with Miss Winover, occasionally meeting her in her professional capacity as a district visitor. The lady was a good type of a class which has perhaps more female than male representatives, because ladies have more time for making proselytes than men. Miss Winover, an unmarried lady with an independent income, was especially well adapted for the profession of an amateur missionary. She was an ultra-strict Catholic. It had never occurred to her to doubt that there was no hope of salvation out of the pale of the Church. Consequently she acted with perfect consistency in attempting to convert others to the true faith.

Doubt or conscientious disbelief was a mental condition which Miss Winover could not comprehend. She was thirty years old, and had received the average education of the middle class. Her mental calibre did not permit her to examine, which would have been a sin, as implying doubt. She had been bred a Catholic, and a Catholic she remained, just as she would have remained a Lutheran, a Calvinist, an Episcopalian, or an adherent of any other religion. Naturally gentle and amiable, she was only unjust and uncharitable in religion. To bring all her friends and acquaintances over to the faith was not merely a duty, but a hobby—a mania. She never went without tracts for distribution, and she never lost an opportunity of trying to make a proselyte, no matter who or what the person might be, from a poor apple-woman to an Anglican dignitary. Miss Winover was not deterred by any mental or social superiority in her opponent for the time being. No matter under what disabilities she laboured, she felt confident in one grand advantage, which made ample amends for all deficiencies—the possession of the true faith. As she was neither learned nor gifted with controversial powers, her zeal often provoked a laugh among her auditors, when she assailed with temerity some scholar or philosopher, who merely replied with the polished weapons of irony.

As already intimated, she had made the acquaintance of Miss Singleton, not long previously, but Miss Winover had, as the Scotch ministers say, "improved the opportunity."

She had as a matter of course set to work to convert Miss Singleton, and was highly pleased at the progress she had made. Though Madeline was in every respect very superior to Miss Winover, the latter soon obtained an influence over her new friend which it is not difficult to explain. Miss Winover had spoken in the highest terms of Father Stirling, without, of course, entertaining the slightest idea that he was the hero of the stories he had narrated on the night of the ball. Madeline naturally found a pleasure in listening to the praises of Clement Stirling. She now heard from the lips of her friend particulars of the life of him whose career in its main events she had already followed. How natural that Miss Winover's self-love should blind her to this innocent deceit of the invalid Madeline; how characteristic in the zealous propagandist to attribute to her own efforts, under Providence, the happy change so rapidly taking place in her friend's religious convictions. Miss Winover was then particularly proud of her proselyte, for she had an affectionate disposition, and it was impossible for her to know Madeline without cherishing towards her love and esteem.

When Father Stirling entered the drawing-room of the house in Upper Berkeley Street which Miss Winover shared with a widow lady, a distant relative, who acted towards her as chaperone and companion, he found Miss Winover seated at the piano with Rossini's *Stabat Mater* before her. She rose immediately on the priest's entrance, and her manner expressed extreme gratification combined with some confusion at so gracious and unexpected a visit. For Miss Winover, as has been already seen, was a devoted admirer of Father Stirling.

Miss Winover was a comely woman of the ordinary height, inclining to stoutness. Her light flaxen hair was gathered behind her head, and confined by a net of blue chenille. She wore a plain morning lavender-coloured stuff dress trimmed with black velvet, and a small richly-carved ebony crucifix depended from her neck by a necklace of jet. Miss Winover did not courtsey as she would have done to an ordinary acquaintance, but inclined before the priest with a lowly and profound genuflexion which lasted about a minute, and seemed to distress Father Stirling. He was pained by this homage to his piety. Yet he did not like to check it, as he knew that Miss Winover took a pleasure in such observances. When the lady at length permitted her eyes to rest upon those of her visitor, she said in tones which faltered a little:

"Is it possible that I behold his Reverence Father Stirling? How can I sufficiently express to your Reverence my sense of the honour your Reverence confers by this visit to my poor house?"

She continued, more like a woman of the world, as she was whenever religion was not concerned:

"But pray be seated. Do, your Reverence, take this arm-chair near the fire, and place your feet on this stool. Will you allow me to offer you some refreshment? Do, your Reverence, try a glass of wine and a biscuit. You have walked, and your health is delicate."

As Father Stirling knew that Miss Winover would have been hurt by a refusal to accept her hospitality, he assented, and the refreshment was placed on the table. After a few common-place observations, Father Stirling referred to the object of his visit. He began—

"I learned the other day in conversation with Father Wiley that there is a young lady, a friend of yours, who—"

Although the priest believed Miss Winover was quite in the dark respecting his previous relations with Miss Singleton, yet such was the effect of conscience, that Father Stirling hesitated to pronounce her name. Miss Winover came unconsciously to his rescue.

"You mean Miss Singleton, do you not?"

"I do," said Father Stirling, very much relieved thus to have got over the difficulty.

"Ah! yes. I have very nearly turned her. If she would but have an interview with a priest, I feel quite confident she would become a Catholic. But do you know I greatly fear that unless some steps are taken soon, it will be too late, and my poor friend may die in her error."

The glass of wine which Father Stirling was raising mechanically to his lips, fell from his hand. Muttering some incoherent words of apology, he bent down as if to pick up the fragments of the broken glass, in reality to hide the evidences of his emotion at these terribly significant words. By a very strong effort of self-restraint, he succeeded in remaining silent, in staying the flood of questions which rose to his lips, and which would have betrayed his secret.

"Oh pray, your Reverence, do not demean yourself to stoop. How can you think of such a trifle? You really distress me," cried Miss Winover, as she rang the bell. "Susannah," she said to the servant who entered, "bring another glass, and then sweep up here."

When the servant had obeyed these orders

and left the room, Father Stirling said, "You really think then, Miss Winover, that Miss Singleton's health is in such a dangerous state?"

"There is not the slightest doubt of it, unfortunately. She received some shock at Lady Oldtowers' ball the other night, where I had the happiness of seeing your Reverence. She has been very unwell ever since. There was some mystery there which she will not disclose. It is quite evident she has something weighing upon her mind. If she were a Catholic she could relieve it under the seal of confession. As it is, she persists in saying that her fainting was caused by the excitement, and the heat of the rooms."

"You are intimate with Miss Singleton?" said Father Stirling, who had now recovered his self-command.

"Oh we are like sisters," replied Miss Winover, "and if you knew her, you would not wonder at the deep sympathy she has awakened in me, and, indeed, in all who are acquainted with her. What agony of mind I have endured, from reflecting that my sweet friend is still a heretic, still spiritually blind, still therefore—alas!—under condemnation. And yet she is almost a Catholic. She listens willingly and with the deepest interest to my humble attempts to point out the right way. I have begun and carried on the good work, which it requires a Divine to accomplish. A priest, I am certain, would have no difficulty in persuading her to abjure the Protestant Heresy. I can assure your Reverence it has cost me many sleepless nights thinking what course I ought to pursue in this critical situation. I have consulted Father Wiley as my spiritual director."

"And what course did he advise?"

"Nothing! That is to say, he said I could do nothing more than I had already done. He said I had acted right in opening Miss Singleton's eyes to her spiritually dangerous state, and that the responsibility now rested with her, for that, if knowing the errors of Protestantism she still remained a Protestant, she would be no longer a *material* but a *formal* heretic. I asked Father Wiley whether I ought not to bring a priest to my dear friend on my own responsibility?"

"And what answer did he make to that question?" said Father Stirling, eagerly, as if a suspicion of Father Wiley's good faith had suddenly darted across his mind.

"He said, no. I must not think of it."

Father Stirling's countenance showed a sense of relief. Miss Winover continued:—

"Father Wiley added there were certain conventionalities and proprieties which we could not set aside, and that we should only do harm and bring down heretical odium on the faith by acting in what would seem so officious a manner. But I can assure your Reverence that my conscience is not at all easy on this matter, and that I cannot bring myself to agree with Father Wiley. Ah! if your Reverence would not think me too bold I would ask for your opinion. If your Reverence would deign to enlighten me with your convictions, all doubt and hesitation would be removed."

Father Stirling was troubled by this reference to himself involving the question which he had been in vain trying to solve. He said, to gain time:

"Surely the opinion of Father Wiley, your spiritual director, should be sufficient."

"It ought to be so, and yet your Reverence must pardon me for saying there are times that I do not feel easy under Father Wiley's direction. My great complaint is that he is too lenient to my sins."

"That is a rare complaint for a penitent to make, Miss Winover," said Father Stirling, endeavouring to assume a jocularity which belied his feelings. "Penitents in general think their confessors too severe."

"Well, your Reverence, it is as I say. I sometimes think it would be better for my soul's health if Father Wiley were more severe. For instance at a ball, a short time since, I forgot and ate after twelve o'clock at night. Horrified at the sin I had been guilty of (for the following day was a fast day), I was in hopes that Father Wiley would have inflicted a proportionately severe penance, that I might mortify the flesh. Yet he only said that, as I had eaten through forgetfulness, I had in fact committed a most venial sin, and that I might consider myself quite absolved by saying an extra *Ave* at evening prayers. And it is not once in a way, but frequently that Father Wiley has shown me this strange leniency. For instance, one Friday, I was dining with a Protestant family, and so far forgot myself as to eat meat. Well, Father Wiley condoned this offence in the same manner. The next time we met he laughed and said: 'Persons who are compelled to associate so much with heretics are often led into venial sins. Both you and I, Miss Winover, are illustrations of this.' Now I do not like this conduct of Father Wiley, and I have reflected that persons who are so ready to grant indulgence to others may not be very strict in their own way of living. Mrs. Chatterly says he is very fond of good eating and drinking, and that his housekeeper is much too young and too pretty."

It will be seen from the above that Miss Winover, like many of the ultra-religious or *unco guid*, had her faults; that she was in short, fond of talking scandal. In this instance her besetting sin had actually rendered her oblivious of the great indiscretion (to use the least opprobrious term) of censuring one clergyman to another.

"But pardon me," she resumed, abruptly, "your Reverence, for running away from the subject of poor, dear Miss Singleton. You must know I had a plan, that is to say, I have ventured to dream of a plan, which would be so nice if it only had the sanction of your Reverence. I have often spoken of your Reverence to Miss Singleton, and she displayed the deepest interest, as was natural, in listening to the details of the self-denying life led by your Reverence."

While Miss Winover was speaking, Father Stirling bent his eyes on the carpet, his disgust at this fulsome praise overpowered by emotion at hearing that Madeline Singleton had heard of him in this way, and curiosity to learn if she had in any way betrayed their mutual secret. Miss Winover continued—

"Fnding my sweet friend took such a lively interest in hearing of your saintly life, an idea came into my head, and I have never been able to get rid of it since. What if Madeline were to come and spend the day with me? What if the excellent and pious Father Stirling were to call on that day, and if his exhortation were to complete the conversion of my friend, if not at the first meeting, on succeeding interviews? She would become a Catholic, and—"

Father Stirling interrupted her, emphatically:—

"This must not be thought of for an instant, Miss Winover."

The lady crossed her hands on her breast and bowed her head humbly, like a nun listening to a reproof from her superior.

"Pardon, Father, if I have offended," she said, meekly. "It was but a dream."

Father Stirling felt sorry that he had spoken so harshly. He continued mildly—

"Your intention was doubtless good, but on this subject I agree with your director. Father Wiley is quite right. If Miss Singleton voluntarily abjures the Protestant religion—"

"*Heresy*, your Reverence," interrupted Miss Winover.

Father Stirling continued—

"If Miss Singleton wishes to change her faith, well and good, but I never càn consent to a conversion brought about by stratagem."

"It is true," said Miss Winover, who could not banish the ruling passion; "that there would be a certain degree of collusion, or, as your Reverence says, stratagem; but is not this (I do not affirm—I merely ask), is not this warrantable under the peculiar circumstances? Have not some of our doctors thought that a deviation from strict literal verity would be pardonable, and even meritorious, to ensure so great a good as the conversion of a heretic, and the salvation of a human soul?"

After she had made this speech, Miss Winover blushed very much. She quailed at her own temerity in actually presuming to argue a case of conscience with a priest, and with such a celebrated priest as Father Stirling. A moment before she had been carried away by her zeal; now she was again the humble devotee, trembling before her spiritual teacher.

Father Stirling replied, seriously—

"I know not where you have learnt such lessons. I can only repeat that your proposition involves a deliberate deceit, and as such would be a grave sin."

"Pray, your Reverence, do not speak so

harshly; I only sought to know your opinion. Since you disapprove of my plan, it must be wrong, and I shall think no more of it. But, at least, I may endeavour to persuade Miss Singleton to ask for an interview. I may tell her what you have said, and if she desires to see you, you will come, will you not, your Reverence?"

"Listen, Miss Winover," said Father Stirling, gravely. "I authorise you to tell Miss Singleton this: that if she conscientiously wishes to join the Catholic Communion, and if she desires my services in doing so, I will come and see her under her father's roof, and, of course, with his sanction. On no other conditions do I authorise you to propose an interview between her and myself, or any other priest."

"Your Reverence shall be implicitly obeyed," said Miss Winover, humbly. "If in my zeal, Father, I would have acted in a manner unworthy of your sanction, I confess my fault, for whatever you say must be right. You have lightened my heart of a heavy load. I have not the slightest doubt that Miss Singleton would gladly see your Reverence, but her father—he, alas! is blinded in his ignorance—one of the most obstinate of heretics. I have heard him speak in such a shocking manner of the Holy Father" (here Miss Winover crossed herself). "Colonel Singleton, I fear, will never consent. And yet, who knows? The prayer of his daughter, it may be her dying prayer, may move even his hardened heart. But, should it be otherwise—"

"Then, God's will be done," said Father Stirling, with quivering lip.

"Amen," said Miss Winover, crossing herself reverently. She continued—

"She must then die a heretic. Is it the opinion of your Reverence that, if, through Colonel Singleton's obstinacy, his daughter be refused the consolation of dying in the profession of the true faith, her soul may yet be saved?"

"Let us sinners forbear to discuss such awful questions," responded the priest, in an agitated voice. "Let us do our duty, and trust to the mercy of God."

Miss Winover again crossed herself, but she could not yet abandon the point.

"Miss Singleton is certainly very amiable, and in her heart I am sure she holds the true faith, and it certainly does not appear to be her fault if her father hinders her from professing according to her wishes; but still, there is the express declaration of Holy Church—against all heretics. Oh, to think of her dying without the last rites of the Church, without confession and extreme unction!"

Miss Winover was evidently very much perplexed between her desire to render obedience to the constituted ecclesiastical authorities, and her own strict theological views; between her confidence in Father Stirling's infallibility, and her firm belief that there could be salvation for none, who died out of the pale of the Catholic Church. In order to change the subject, Father Stirling said—

"I learned from Father Wiley that Miss Singleton had spent some time in a Protestant religious house."

This remark was quite enough to start Miss Winover on a new phase of her mania. She went off at once into a description of the Protestant Nunnery, where Miss Singleton had spent a year. Though Father Stirling had no sympathy with the tone in which she spoke, he could not help listening with avidity to every detail relative to Miss Singleton, and soon found himself deeply interested in Miss Winover's narrative.

BOOK IV.

CHAPTER I.

PROTESTANT NUNNERIES.

As has been already implied, Miss Singleton had not found happiness or contentment since the rupture of her engagement with Clement Stirling. Hers, however, were not merely the sufferings of a woman disappointed in love. From that cause she did indeed suffer much, as she had dearly loved Clement Stirling. But it subsequently appeared that his spoken and written arguments had taken much more effect than she imagined at the time. Madeline pondered over them for years, and had been slowly but surely growing more and more inclined to her lover's religious views. The bluff Colonel, her father, was like many other men, a staunch Protestant, without being able to satisfy scruples of conscience which he himself had never felt and could not comprehend. Then the career of Clement Stirling had naturally a great effect on Madeline. Her true woman's heart was delighted to learn that her former lover had found that peace which was denied to herself. The reports of his zealous, useful, noble life, his great fame as a preacher, had caused her sincere, *disinterested* gratification, for she knew that these things aided to build up the barrier between them in this world. Once she had gone to hear him preach, and the effect of his eloquence was so decided, that probably the only reason for not joining the Romish Communion was her strong sentiment of filial duty. Miss Winover was not wrong in saying that Miss Singleton was at heart a Catholic.

In her attempts to find peace, to stay the

battle of conscience, Madeline had at last wrung from her father a reluctant consent to join for a year a Protestant Sisterhood, which had been recently established in London.* Miss Proctor, the lady who presided over this establishment, was a well-intentioned woman, and had begun well. She however illustrated the danger of entrusting any human being with arbitrary power. At first the Sisters had been most active agents in the distribution of charity and in nursing the sick. It was found convenient to adopt the conventual costume. This had the desired effect of enabling them to pass unmolested, without misconception or insult, through scenes which they could not otherwise have visited with impunity. Gradually, however, with the conventual dress crept in conventual discipline, vows of implicit obedience to the superior, vows of silence, fasting, and other pen-

* The author must here apologise for taking some liberties with chronology. So far as he is aware, the establishment of Sisterhoods and Nunneries in the Anglican Church is of more recent date A beginning was made about the year 1848, and there are now about twenty-five of these establishments throughout England.

ances injurious to the health. This Sisterhood, once so useful, so practically charitable, and whose members had been so happy, ere Madeline entered it, was a complete Catholic convent—only more so! That is to say, it was copiously encrusted with all the evils of a Catholic convent, without its advantages, ameliorations, and impediments to the abuse of authority. Its rules were in many respects more stringent, more distressing to the mind and body; and, as it was not recognised by the ecclesiastical authorities, it was subject to no supervision of any kind, either from a clergyman or a magistrate. The consequences may be imagined. While continually crying out against the encroachments of Rome, we are permitting the organization of Protestant Nunneries! far worse conducted than Romish Convents.*

* The following, headed, "Extraordinary Clerical Proceedings," is the account of a Sister taking the veil in All Saints' Church, Margaret Street, London. "The Sisters entered first, and knelt down and continued kneeling through the whole service, which lasted more than two hours. The Clergy then entered, and after lighting the candles on the altar, proceeded to celebrate the Holy Communion. A sermon was preached, in which the 'Sacrament' of monastic vows was highly eulogized, and seemed to be preferred to Baptism, the Eucharist, 'Penance,' and the

Miss Proctor, from the unassuming head of a Charitable Sisterhood was transformed into a Mother Superior, a Lady Abbess, a Popess, in short an irresponsible autocrat over her little flock of good but silly women. Each sister on joining was obliged to take, in the most solemn manner, a vow of "Holy obedience" to her Spiritual Mother. They were "children" looking to her for everything. But Miss Proctor was gradually ceasing to exert a mother's care. She became every day more wedded to religious duties, that is to say, more given to prayer, alone with the only clergyman ever admitted within the walls of

'other Sacraments.' After the Communion Service, the new Sister, arrayed as a bride, proceeded to answer a long series of questions, from which it appeared she was taking the vows voluntarily, and that they were to bind her for one year. At the end of that time, which, as in the Romish Church, is considered the noviciate, she will, if so disposed, assume the black veil and become bound for life. After the examination the habit of a novice was displayed, and the officiating clergyman or 'father,' as he was termed, blessed the various garments, and the novice withdrawing, put off her bridal dress, and assumed the habit. The other sisters then kissed her in turns, saying—'Bless thee, sister ——.' Then followed deep obeisances to the Lady Superior and to 'Father — —,' who conducted the service. It was now considered that the novice had been married to the church, and, therefore, the whole party adjourned to a wedding breakfast, provided with the orthodox wedding cake, and wanting only in the rather essential constituent of a bridegroom. The bridal party seemed very merry, though we doubt whether the 'Father' would be so were the bishop of London aware of those proceedings of a clergyman of the Church of England."—*Western Morning News.*

the convent. This was Tractarian Doctor Formula, who was by the Low Church party compared to a guide-post, pointing the way and directing others to Rome, without going thither himself. There are not a few men now in the Church of England who are Papist in everything but the name. Why, then, ask simple people, don't they become Roman Catholic priests at once? Simply because a bird in the hand is worth two in the bush. The actual stipends which they receive from the Church which they betray, are considerably more than the possible emolument they might receive from the Pope. But it is to be presumed that these Jesuits calm their consciences with the reflection that they are doing Rome good service, indirectly, if not openly, by the crop of semi-Papists, which they are sowing, and then it is quite right for the Children of Israel to spoil the Egyptians. This may appear severe. I ask is it not true? Are not these Jesuits in disguise doing far more harm than avowed Jesuits can do? because the former are the accepted, recognized, State-appointed teachers of the people.

As the Mother Superior became wrapt in religious observances, in prayer and meditation, she became less attentive to the duties of charity and the comforts of her "children," and more alive to the comforts of herself and the Spiritual Director, Doctor Formula. The business of the house was carried on by deputies, called Eldresses, who strictly enforced the ascetic rules on the Sisters. The "children" had no fires in their cells, but the apartments occupied by the Spiritual Mother and the Director were heated by hot-air pipes. The Sisters slept in bare unfurnished cells, but the rooms of the Spiritual Mother and the Director were luxuriously (and those of the Eldresses comfortably) furnished. The Sisters were half-starved in obedience to the vow of Holy Poverty, but the Spiritual Mother and the Director dispensed themselves from the strict observance of those vows. Doubtless *their* superior piety no longer needed abstinence—nay, required good living. The Sisters infringed the rule if they answered a civil question, or even so much as looked at a man in the street; but the Spiritual Mother and the Director lived in the enjoyment of platonic friendship.

Nor was this all. Selfish indifference to the comforts of others, under the religious garb, the strange pleasure of making others fast and toil, while the Mother Superior breaks the rules she imposes upon the poor fools who obey her, do not stop at inconvenience. There is a darker side to the picture. Sins of omission may be carried to a criminal extent. Some of the Sisters were permitted to commit gradual suicide, by fasting until their strength sank under the deprivation. One sister, from this cause, and through getting wet feet from the want of shoes, for which she asked in vain, caught a cold which settled on her lungs. Everything in the house went on as usual; prayers, chapel service, and religious exercises of various kinds during the greater part of the day, and even in the middle of the night. Some of the Sisters who had not become mere automata pitied sister Theresa; but they could do nothing, and the Spiritual Mother never sent for a doctor. Immersed in her religious meditations Miss Proctor had never probably observed how ill her "child" was. Sister Theresa was allowed to have a fire. She was also allowed to drag up long flights of stairs to her cell the coals to make the fire. Although daily growing weaker, she never complained. She had been taught to believe that this process of suicide to which she, at least, was the innocent accomplice and victim, was a certain path to eternal glory. At length the poor suffering creature died. Ought there not to have been an inquest on her body? What would have been the verdict of such an inquest? She had the mockery of a splendid funeral. She, who had wanted shoes while she lived, and other necessaries and attendance, which would have kept her alive; she who had been permitted to droop and die in this "religious" house; she who would have been saved in a public hospital; she who had died *almost alone* and without the sisters in general knowing of it, was laid in a costly coffin, covered with a pall of glittering white and gold, with a cross upon her breast!

Would Sister Theresa have died had she lived in the wicked world, where she might have known the care of a natural, not a spiritual and unnatural mother? If Miss Proctor had been a mother she might have been more human! In her case the strictest religious observances did not supply the place of this holy instinct of nature. Alas, the mother of Sister Theresa had died of grief from parting with her only child, who had been too effectually taught that it was piety to be disobedient to her own mother, and to choose another parent instead of the one given her by God.

Whether Miss Singleton was more independent than the other "children," or more penetrating, and could not admire the selfishness of the Mother Superior, her despotic rule, her silly affectations of dress and manner; or whether Miss Proctor had taken offence at the Colonel's manifest unwillingness to leave his daughter in her care, an evident coldness existed between her and Madeline. Colonel Singleton had asked that his daughter might leave the establishment when she chose. The Mother Superior seemed deeply offended at the proposal, and informed the colonel that no sister could take the vows for less than a year. Colonel Singleton then asked permission to see his daughter when he chose. This was also refused as an infraction of their laws. Sisters were not permitted to see their relatives unless in cases of extreme illness; but, as already said, Sister Theresa had died without the presence of any of her relatives. He might receive letters from his daughter, but the vow of holy obedience obliges all letters received or sent, to be shown to the superior; consequently it is *she* who speaks, writes, and acts for her "child."

The discipline of the house was far too severe for Madeline's state of health. Yet for her there was no relaxation. If at times her natural good sense led her to suspect that this mode of life was very far from the ideal of religion she had pictured to herself; if the universal instinctive perception of injustice taught her the evils of the system, and she felt a wish to appeal against them, to whom was she to complain? The bishop of the diocese never visited the institution. The clergyman of the parish disapproved, but could do nothing. Doctor Formula, the spiritual director, treated all complaints as a spiritual falling away from grace. Madeline was at length sent back to her father, almost in a dying state. Her constitution was seriously weakened by the life of asceticism, and there is little doubt that had she remained much longer in this "religious house" she would have died. One lady, of independent fortune, who had joined the Sisterhood against the wish of her parents, died there, and left the whole of her property to the society, or in fact to the Mother Superior, who had unlimited control of the funds. The lady, though adjured by her relatives to return to them, had been retained in the nunnery by her vow of holy obedience, and by the fear of being refused absolution by the spiritual director. Her parents, therefore, had the consolation of knowing that their daughter's wealth had gone to enrich those who had robbed them of their child!

As may be imagined, some very warm words passed between Colonel Singleton and Miss Proctor; but he could do nothing beyond cross-questioning his daughter and making as public as possible the sufferings entailed by the disgraceful mismanagement of the Sisterhood. Miss Proctor, who probably despaired of getting Miss Singleton's fortune, did not wish her to die in the convent, and (as Madeline was not so stupid and tractable as the rest of the sisters) declared that Miss Singleton had no vocation for a "religious" life. What humility! To call obedience to Miss Proctor a *religious* life.

CHAPTER II.

CONVENTUAL ASCETICISM.

Is it not evident that Sisterhoods, modelled on this system, approach the Jesuit type? Their vows are almost the same. The following is an extract from the rule of holy obedience of the Devonport Sisters, from Miss Goodman's work: — "Actions, in themselves indifferent, become sanctified when done in the spirit of holy obedience, for all authority descends from God, and *Superiors bear the image of the divine power of God, which He vouchsafes to imprint upon them. And He will surely require it at your hands if ye despise His authority in them.* Cherish *and obey her* (the spiritual mother) with holy love, *without any murmur or sign of hesitation or repugnance*, but simply, cordially, and promptly obey with cheerfulness, *and banish from your mind any question as to the wisdom of the command given you!* One who is obedient will obey readily, serving God. She seeks for no reason, asks not the end of the command, but tranquilly, and in peace, applies her ears to hear every precept, and her hands and feet instantly to fulfil it." Has not this the direct tendency of Loyola's command of implicit obedience, namely, to destroy the human will, and make the individual a living corpse in the hands of the Superior?

I am totally misapprehended if the above remarks are construed into an attack on Sisterhoods of Charity as such. All honour to those worthy women who band together to assist the poor, to succour the distressed, to alleviate the bed of pain and sickness. It is a matter of no importance to me whether such associations are Protestant or Catholic. They are of a far higher order than the Conventual, as I think is testified by actual experience. I will instance but one out of the many noble charities of the Roman Church—the Sisters of St. Vincent de Paul. Their founder, St. Vincent, said:—"Your title will be, 'Sisters of Charity, Servants of the Sick Poor. Oh! beautiful name! beautiful employment! Oh! my daughters, what have you done for God to merit the glorious title—Servants of the Poor? It is as if we said, servants of Jesus Christ, because He reckons as done to Himself all that is done for His members. The streets of the city, or the houses of the sick, shall be your cloister: hired rooms shall be your cells; your chapel shall be the parish church; obedience shall be your solitude; the fear of God your grating; and a strict and holy modesty your only veil."

Let us not confound associations such as this with conventual institutions. It may be said both monasteries and convents supply a necessary want, and do good. How can a man or woman best attain to real happiness? By the unalloyed pleasure of doing good to our fellow-creatures. How can we best benefit our fellow-creatures? Not by shutting ourselves up in cells and caves; by leading the life of a hermit, a recluse; by consuming our days in a petty round of puerile observances; but by going forth into the world, by acting, suffering, learning to sympathise with men and women, by accepting our share of the struggle and the toil of existence. To live in the world well and nobly is more courageous, more religious, than to immure oneself within a monastery or convent. But it is urged—the world is full of wickedness; of temptations to sin. Granted! How shall we avoid sin; By flight or conquest? Let us raise our eyes to Jesus. What was the example set by Him? did He fly from the world? Did He avoid temptation? Did He dwell alone? Did He despair of man's welfare or regeneration? Did He shut himself up in a religious house? Jesus did none of these things. And the true Christian hero is he who battles in the arena of the world, who tries to make his fellow-men better than they are, by precept and example.

But it is urged, many of us are too weak for the sore struggle. The conflict is too unequal. The world would contaminate, absorb, conquer, and destroy us. The plea of expediency is indeed the only excuse which should be urged for conventual institutions. It admits that the life of the anchorite and the nun is not the highest life. But at the same time it is a just plea. For exactly as it would be inhuman to force the frail, the infirm, the afflicted, to fight by the side of the able-bodied soldier, so would it be morally wrong to force the spiritually weak into temptation. There are occasions in which to avoid the trial which appears too strong for us, argues true moral courage. From this point of view a great deal may be said in favour of conventual institutions. They are in fact, as human nature is constituted, necessary evils. The repression of the monasteries by Henry VIII. was both a crime and a mistake. They should have been reformed, and subjected to strict supervision—not suppressed. Voluntary charities are far preferable to the work-house! We should make due allowance for the modification of human temperaments and character. Some of us are so constituted that we can abstain from a thing altogether, but cannot indulge in moderation. Such may require the severe restraints of the monastic and conventual system. Some are left without ties to make life very interesting. The visions of youth are gone—without parents, wife, husband, brother, sister, or children, the world appears to them one huge wilderness. Such a one is already an involuntary anchorite, monk, or nun.

Should we try to hinder such a one from seeking out other persons similarly situated—from finding (what we all desire) sympathy from their common misfortunes, from living together, "the world forgetting, by the world forgot"—would you not permit those old men or old women to wait for their respective summonses to a better world in one of those calm retreats, these secluded refuges which were so popular in the middle ages?

Heaven forbid that we should deny the weary soul the privilege of escape from out the boiling, surging rapids in the river of life, into one of the calm eddies of religious meditation. But what I raise my voice against, is, binding the conscience by an irrevocable vow, consigning the young to an ascetic life—a living tomb. How dastardly to take advantage of some temporary disgust with life, such as we all at some time or other experience! A young lady has met with a disappointment of the heart, or is not quite happy because she does not know her own mind, and has not yet had sufficient experience to make principle and practice agree. Should she, on that account, take a vow of perpetual celibacy, or be permitted to shut herself up in a religious house—all the grand and noble ends of life, the proper employment of her energies denied her—the smiling face of nature, with its sweet flowers, and song of birds, and other joyous and beautiful things, hidden by the conventual veil?

Why indulge a romantic, sentimental young lady, coquetting with melancholy, to believe that she will find no happiness but in the cloister? If a lady thinks she has a vocation for this life, let her try it, but on the express understanding that her vows are not to extend beyond a certain definite period; and let every care be taken by her relatives and friends that she be at perfect liberty, if she choose, to return to the harmless pleasures of the world; that no undue means be used by the sisterhood to influence her decision, and that there be not the slightest stigma of disgrace in abandoning a conventual life. For want of these proper precautions, not a few unfortunate women are now kept in spiritual bondage in Protestant as well as Catholic nunneries. A lady who once used these arguments to an old nun was answered, "You would then give none but the dry, withered sticks to the Lord?" This reply embodies a fallacy which lies at the bottom of spiritual asceticism, whatever form it takes, and wherever it appears—the fallacy that God wishes his creatures to be unhappy. It is astonishing to see what primitive and barbarous ideas still pervade our civilization! Jephthah thought it a religious act to sacrifice his daughter to the Lord. From the same mistaken principle Agamemnon was forced to sacrifice Iphigenia. It was thought, and it is still thought, that to sacrifice something very precious to us, either our own children, or our own love of harmless pleasures, will render the Deity propitious.

Such an idea can be traced in the sacrifices of all nations, and all times, and it is still powerful in the conventual system, and the infliction of penances. The principle is the same in all asceticism, but it undergoes modification according to the greater or less degree of civilization. Thus, the Indian devotee throws himself under the wheels of the car of Juggernaut, or is suspended by a hook which lacerates his flesh, or gashes himself with knives. A European devotee macerates or flagellates himself, wears a hair shirt, and refrains from food. The same idea actuates both—that God is pleased and appeased by human suffering; that Heaven is to be gained by self-inflicted tortures, either of the mind or body, or both.

I do not deny that, of the two extremes, asceticism is better than self-indulgence; but both are faults. Our appetites, our mental and physical desires were bestowed to be exercised with moderation. Temperance does not consist in their annihilation, but in their subjection. And what does the ascetic system proceed from? An unnatural slavish, selfish fear for our own salvation. Always for ourselves; not compassion for the world at large; but a terrible dread, amounting at times to madness, that the soul of the devotee is doomed to everlasting perdition. To avert this doom the monastic ascetic spends the day in repeating prayers, which, from their frequency, must cease to impress the mind; in maintaining strict silence rules; in making the sign of the cross, and bowing reverently to the superior. What is the difference between the ascetic monk or nun, and the inmate of a lunatic asylum? This—that the latter may be *happy!*

CHAPTER III.

FATHER STIRLING'S HEAVY TRIAL.

Now began for the unfortunate priest a trial of a truly horrible nature. Through the secret machinatious of Wiley, about a week after the dinner at his house, Dr. Hood, his ecclesiastical superior, signified to Father Stirling that he must resume the duties of the confessional. This was a part of his parochial duties for which the priest had the greatest aversion, and was indeed the only portion of duty which he may be said to have neglected. This neglect had hitherto been winked at, owing to the sense of Father Stirling's great services in other respects. Dr. Hood represented to him that in consequence of an intimation he had received from the bishop, he was compelled to request Father Stirling's resumption of this duty. When Father Stirling first entered the confessional, he had endeavoured to confine himself to the poor, but this was now impossible. His reputation caused him to be in great request. He became a fashionable confessor. And what was the preparation for the confessional? It will be no news to many of my readers to tell them that the professional education of the priest involves, like that of the surgeon or physician, the making acquaintance with some of the most painful subjects. The Catholic church considers the priest as father, physician, doctor, and judge. The theory then is, there is no more danger to the priest in becoming acquainted with these things, than what is run in the practice of the law and medicine, as the lawyer and the physician are both called upon to treat of the most indelicate matters. This, however, does not appear to me a correct analogy. The theory, however plausible, breaks down in practice. Society can spare the confessor far better than the doctor or the lawyer, though it would be a happy day when it could spare all three.

The reason why Father Stirling never had the treatise, "*De usu matrimonii*," put into his hand before, was, a deference to the opinion of Father Wiley, who knew his pupil's disposition well, and saw the danger of alarming his purity until time and habit had done their work on the conscience, and made him a faithful servant of Rome. The effect which it had upon the mind of Father Stirling may be imagined from the following graphic sketch: *

"Let us suppose the case of a young bachelor priest placed in a large parish: at a time when he was unable to form a decided opinion whether he possessed the gift of celibacy or not, he was led to vow eternal dedication to that state; he is instructed in

* Awful Disclosures, or Extracts from the Moral Theology of Alphonsius Liguori, with Remarks by the Rev. R. P. Blakeney, B.A.

such treatises as that on 'the use of matrimony,' to which we have directed attention, and of which Liguori himself says, that it is sufficient to 'disturb pure minds.' He is conscientious, he struggles under the yoke which was imposed upon him, and sighs beneath the corruptions of the heart, which is described by inspired men as being 'deceitful above all things, and desperately wicked,' the carnal propensities of which are drawn out and inflamed by the foul and obscene treatises in which he is instructed; he groans beneath the wickedness of his nature and exclaims, 'Oh, wretched man that I am; who shall deliver me from the body of this death?' He is at length convinced that the way to avoid unholy thoughts, is to avoid those things which suggest them; he determines that henceforth he will not think or speak of the things that are done of them in secret, but obey the apostolic injunction, 'Finally, brethren, whatsoever things are true, whatsoever things are honest, whatsoever things are just, whatsoever things are pure, whatsoever things are lovely, whatsoever things are of good report, if there be any virtue, if there be any praise, think on these things.' With righteous indignation he casts the unholy book from him; he feels that impurity is in its contents. Wretched man! the remembrance of his eternal vow seizes upon him—he must either approve of the duties of the confessor's office, or become in his estimation a wretched, perjured, sacrilegious heretic. He must go forward—penitents of every grade and condition present themselves; his time is for the most part occupied in hearing confessions. Now in private he is brought into personal contact with sinners of every kind—the sins of which before he had only read are now poured out by *human* lips, into a *human* heart—all secrets are made known; unchastity, in all its varieties, and with all its circumstances, is minutely detailed; the young, the lovely, pour into his yet tender heart every emotion—the debauched, the profligate, the unchaste are there to make known their guilty state. Thus he listens to, and is bound to elicit, the most unholy thoughts; he is brought into private, personal contact with all his parishioners, and that constantly. The wife tells the secrets of her husband—aye, secrets, peradventure, which the husband knows not. Mothers, wives, daughters, sisters, make confessions of which the children, the husbands, the fathers, the brothers know nothing. The things that are done in a world that 'lieth under the wicked one,' are here fully and freely canvassed.

Let the reader imagine what were the emotions of the good and pure Father Stirling, when he first read this book of Liguori, which will never be translated, for the simple reason that any bookseller who should publish an English translation would immediately render himself liable to be indicted under Lord Campbell's Act. His ecclesiastical superior said to him, on putting the book into his hand, "You have been now labouring zealously as a priest for eight years. Your experience of human nature has been great, but as you are comparatively new to the confessional, you may find things in this book which will shock you, which will open up to your horrified gaze, novel aspects of the hideous depravity which marks the original state of man born in sin. You are considerably older than priests in general when they first read this treatise; and you have amply proved that *you* can read it with safety. The object of going with such minute detail into the mysteries of nature, &c., is to prevent the penitent from dwelling needlessly on such matters. 'To the pure all things are pure.' Nevertheless, it would be superfluous to tell you to read it with fervent prayer. Unfortunately, breaches of the sixth and ninth commandments* form the most frequent and abundant matter of confessions. In the words of the accom-

* The reader will bear in mind that the sixth and ninth commandments of the Romish Church are respectively the seventh and a portion of the tenth among Protestants.

plished and pious author, 'let the readers put away all curiosity, and at the same time let them more frequently elevate the mind to God, and commend themselves to the Immaculate Virgin, lest while they desire to gain souls for God they themselves lose their own souls.' "

The mind of a good priest may be compared to that of a pure woman. It should be preserved free from all taint, else the bloom readily rubs off. Men earnestly desire to believe in the virtue of women and of priests, as connecting links, both of them between this world and a more heavenly state. Father Stirling did indeed feel the necessity of prayer on casting his eyes over that treatise of Liguori. "*De usu Matrimonii.*" He had no conception that it was necessary for a man of God to know such inexpressibly vile things. He passed the greater part of that night on his knees before the crucifix, and when his housekeeper brought up his breakfast in the morning she was terrified at his haggard looks.

At the end of six weeks Father Stirling had changed so much that his friends thought he was going into a consumption. The abominable book had the usual effect. It had excited ideas and feelings which the priest had hitherto been able to regulate. The lusts of the flesh were warring against his religious vows. Horrified and ashamed, Father Stirling imposed penance upon penance, each more severe than the preceding. He macerated himself; he wore a belt with iron spikes, and a hair shirt. He endeavoured by every possible means to silence the claims of nature, which appeared to him in the light of a deadly sin. At length these terrible trials resulted in such a failure of health that he felt the necessity of having recourse to the best medical advice.

One day, Hannah, the old housekeeper, entering the priest's room, saw a gentleman standing with his back to her. She was a good deal puzzled to know how this gentleman could have entered the house, for she had not been summoned to the door. She, however, advanced to address the supposed visitor, when he turned round. Hannah had got as far as "His Reverence must have gone out, sir. What name shall I say? ——" when the gentleman smiled, and Hannah, on looking closer, recognised Father Stirling himself. No wonder that the good woman had found a difficulty in recognising the priest, who was dressed in complete secular costume. Although very pale, he looked considerably younger than in his clerical habit. Hannah wondered, but said nothing. Indeed, the worthy old soul, on reflection, felt a little pleased at this metamorphosis. Being a strict Protestant, she thought it not unlikely that Father Stirling might be undergoing the process of conversion to the true faith, and that the change of costume might be symbolical of a change of opinion.

Not to keep the reader in suspense, the true explanation was this: Father Stirling was about to call on a physician. Under the peculiar circumstances of the case, the idea struck him very forcibly that he might both spare his feelings, and receive a more correct knowledge of the actual state of his health, by assuming a harmless incognito. Independently of these motives, it was characteristic of the man to avoid notoriety, as far as possible, and he was frequently distressed on being recognised by persons who had seen him in the pulpit.

CHAPTER IV.

THE RESULTS.

The physician, a man who was celebrated both for his professional skill and his singular independence of mind, and whom I shall call Doctor Blunt, was a middle-aged man, with a spacious brow, an expressive and prepossessing countenance, and a kind and genial, though somewhat abrupt manner. He began by indirect questioning to draw from Father Stirling an account of the nature and causes of his disposition. The doctor asked if his patient had any serious cause of disquietude, remarking that the mind and body were so inscrutably, but, at the same time, so intimately connected, that it was difficult for a doctor to satisfy himself as to the true nature of an ailment without being as inquisitive as a father confessor. He then said, still speaking in a light, jocular manner—

"May I inquire, sir, whether you are a married man?"

Father Stirling replied in the negative.

"No, a jolly bachelor! Eh—"

Father Stirling hesitated. The doctor went on, quite mistaking the cause of this hesitation—

"Come, my dear sir, see in me your father confessor. 'Open confession is good for the soul.' We doctors laugh at the laws of the land. We insist upon the patient criminating himself." He added—

"Believe me, frankness is best. I ask you these questions, because it is impossible for me to tell from your appearance whether your ill-health proceeds from living too fast or too slow. May I inquire your age, sir?"

"Thirty-two."

The physician proceeded to question his patient as to his avocations, whether sedentary or the reverse; whether he studied much, and other particulars relating to his habits. He then said—

"Yes; the case is quite clear. The moral and intellectual qualities, the sentiments cultivated entirely at the expense of the propensities. This will never do. Pray have you never thought about marrying?"

"No, Sir!"

"Then, my dear sir, the best advice I can give you is to begin to think about it. Frankly, there is nothing the matter with you that marriage will not cure. You have been defrauding Nature of her rights, and that good lady is extremely jealous of any interference with her laws. Oh!" continued the doctor, warming with his subject: "when will man learn to live according to the laws of Nature so plainly written down for his observance? Absorbed in your studies, led away by some absorbing ambition, some one engrossing thought (for I read all this in your countenance, independently of what you tell me);

you have hitherto slighted the tender relations, and the present state of your health is the consequence. It will not do, believe me, sir; it will not do. Man is a compound of matter and spirit; of appetite, as well as thought and sentiment, and you have been living as though you were all spirit; as though you had no cerebellum. Whether Combe is physiologically justified in mapping out the brain into distinct organisms I do not know; (I think not, but I belong to the old school); but this I do know, that man is an animal and has a cerebellum. Why then does not man live like an animal as he is? that is, enjoy all his appetites in moderation. Instead of which, men are always in extremes, either in indulging or restraining their passions. Some men live like beasts. No, not like beasts; that is a mere vulgar similitude; beasts never get drunk, or eat, or do anything to excess, that is—beasts in a state of Nature as their Creator made them. But man is always thinking he can improve on Nature. Look at prize sheep and oxen, ugh! I tell you, sir, as I tell all my patients, that when man wanders from the observance of Nature's precepts —no matter in what direction—he commits a sin. There is a confounded school of moral philosophers who write as if the mind were everything, and the body nothing. Pray then, I ask those gentry, did not God make the body as well as the mind? Is not man excellent in every way, whether we consider his mental or physical attributes? Are not all the instincts of Nature right and proper? But these wiseacres forsooth will improve on Nature. They will suppress man's carnal appetites. The fools! why don't they give man's body, this wonderful piece of Divine mechanism, its due place and consideration? If they would do so, they would be far nearer the truth; and by adopting a natural standard man is not such an enormous failure, nor his creation such an egregrious blunder as he appears to them, and the simpletons who read their works in search of truth. But pardon this digression, my dear sir. Believe me, the brain must not be overtasked. We don't live wholly in our moral and intellectual attributes. A man is not perfect till he has loved. It is impossible for a man to love any one woman too well, if he marries and makes her a good husband. This sublime passion leads to conjugal and paternal affection, to the family life, to the sweetest of experiences, the domestic virtues. Believe me, it was never intended for man to live without woman. The man who can dispense with the love of a woman must be either a saint or a sage! He must be strengthened and made altogether independent of the chief solace of human woes, by the direct influence of the Divine love, or his heart shrivelled and ossified at the expense of the brain, must be rendered totally impervious to passion by the undue culture of the intellect. The men who fulfil these conditions through a life-time may be counted on your fingers."

Here the doctor terminated his harangue,

and Father Stirling withdrew. Having paid deep attention and retained every word, he felt too much impressed to prolong the interview. He felt pleased that he had obtained a candid opinion, which he thought might not have been the case had he gone as a priest. But on the other hand that opinion was to him like a funeral knell. He repeated to himself again and again the doctor's concluding words: "The man who can dispense with the love of woman must be either a saint or a sage!" "Ah!" said Father Stirling, "since I am far from being either a saint or a sage, what am I to do?" He pondered deeply over his siugular position, till at length the thought occurred that perhaps an entire change of mental occupation might produce the desired effect. It was a modification of the doctor's idea, that a man must either by the strength of devotional feeling be raised out of the vortex of human passions, or, through the experience of these sublime mental resources which await the exercise of the pure intellect, be enabled to subdue them. Father Stirling said: "Since then, owing to sin, my religious feelings are too weak to banish these assaults of the devil, let me try whether I can find some aid in science."

He returned to the doctor a few days after his first visit. He informed the physician that it was quite impossible to take the remedy he had suggested; that circumstances which he would rather not divulge made marriage an impossibility, and then he waited anxiously to hear what the doctor would say. The doctor remained silent until Father Stirling somewhat nervously said:—

"Is there no other remedy you can suggest?"

The doctor replied with a merry twinkle in his eye, in such a way that even Father Stirling could no longer misunderstand the implication. He started involuntarily, and looked at the physician earnestly, while the latter returned his fixed gaze with an expression in which wonder and pity were mingled. It was the look of the man-of-the-world, regarding one whom he deems particularly "green." It is singular, but true, that the virtue which is prized most in woman, is ridiculed in man.

"Sir," said the priest, forgetting his assumed *incognito*; "Is it possible that you can recommend to me such a breach of morality?"

"My dear Sir," said the doctor, drily, "why so warm? I am not your religious, but your medical adviser. I regard the question entirely from a professional point of view. You come to me with your health greatly undermined, and ask my advice as to the best means of restoring it. Were I an unprincipled humbug, an impudent quack, I would rob and murder you by inches, by giving you drugs, which could do you no manner of good. Instead of that, I come at once to the point. I say marry. You reply, it is impossible to marry. I am sorry to hear it. You then ask for some other remedy, and I tell you the only remedy. Do you think, if I did not think the case absolutely imperative, I would give you this advice? And I will add that if any other medical man (I don't care who he be) gives you other advice, he is imposing on you."

"Sir," said Father Stirling, gravely; "I believe I should ask your pardon, for not having previously informed you that I am a Catholic Priest."

The doctor looked very much astonished at this announcement, which operated an immediate and entire change in his manner.

"I see," he said, in a tone of great feeling, which contrasted remarkably with his former jocular way of speaking, "that this is a much more complicated case than I at first imagined it to be." Father Stirling said hastily: "Would it not be possible, by an entire change of studies, so to divert my mind as to conquer this—this rebellion of the flesh?" The doctor replied slowly: "It might certainly have that effect. It is worth trying. A complete alteration of habits would be beneficial. You must beware of reading too much, but, if you can—thoroughly change the subject of your reading."

The doctor proceeded to apologize for having unwittingly shocked Father Stirling's moral sense. The Priest interrupted him. "It is *I*, Sir, who have to apologize to you, for not having come in my true character. To prove to you that it was from no want of confidence in you, I will at once inform you of my real name." And the Priest gave the doctor a card on which was engraved, "The Reverend Clement Stirling." The doctor could not suppress a slight emotion of supprise when he learnt who his patient was; for the eminent Catholic preacher was well known to him by report. In these days, however, photographs had not made the features of every celebrity familiar. He declined the customary payment, proffered by the Priest, at parting, saying:—"Pardon me, Rev. Sir, from you I can take no fee."

CHAPTER V.

DOUBT AND DESPAIR.

FATHER STIRLING's illness produced one good effect. It was the cause of his studying the Science of Geology. This Science, so recent and yet so important, was then making rapid strides, and working a moral revolution in public opinion. Its deductions, susceptible of the most uncompromising scrutiny and satisfactory proof, have been in too many instances disputed and attacked by the clergy with more zeal than discretion. To these, however, there have been some eminent exceptions—such as Dr. Pye Smith; Archdeacon Pratt; Dr. Buckland; and others. Theology is fighting with Science, in the nineteenth century, a battle similar to that waged in the sixteenth. Then, the cause of strife was Astronomy. Now, it is Geology.

Father Stirling had hitherto accepted implicitly the teaching of the Church. The account of the Creation, given in Genesis, now appeared to him quite at variance with the revelations of Geology. It seemed to him, that in the works written to reconcile Science and Scripture, the authors took unwarrantable liberties with the Sacred text, and thereby made the inspired writer say things which were at variance with legitimate construction. It appeared to him that the Mosaic Cosmogony did assert that this world and the whole universe were created in seven days of our time. He could not deny that this was the popular belief, and it seemed to him that, but for Geology, no one would ever have questioned this belief. He adopted the conclusion of scientific men; that the world has been in existence for immense ages. Father Stirling, in common with other intelligent Catholics, held that when the Church persecuted Galileo, for saying that the Earth moved round the Sun, she had exceeded the authority committed to her, by deciding on a matter of pure science—and had in consequence been deserted by the Spirit of truth! Her decision on this point was therefore, not, infallible. Yet Protestants, who easily get over the difficulties of Astronomy, still teach in their schools that the Earth is a little less than six thousand years old! The conclusion which pressed upon Father Stirling was, that the Bible was not intended to teach scientific truth; that its writers were liable to err when they wrote of things of their own knowledge, and not as inspired men. In short, that the doctrine of the plenary inspiration of the Bible must be abandoned!

Here, then, was a Catholic Priest beginning to think for himself—using the right of private judgment; behaving in short—according to the definition of the Romish Church—like a Heretic and Protestant. Father

Stirling did not stop here. He began to reflect how little he, a minister of Christ, actually knew! He could read the gospels in Greek; but he was not accquainted with the Hebrew language. He accepted the vulgate on the authority of the Church. But here a grave doubt assailed him. The Jews had their learned men, as well as the Christians; and, surely, there is a *primâ facie* evidence, that the Jews can understand their own scriptures as well, if not better than, the Gentiles. In short, Father Stirling, pursuing this train of thought, began to have grave doubts, how far the authority of Rome could relieve him from the privilege or right of thinking for himself.

He saw then the actual prosaic aspect of the life he had chosen. The Priest, in order to be happy, must have no doubts—no misgivings. Father Stirling asked himself whether he was naturally fitted for the profession he had chosen. He saw himself "cabin'd, cribb'd, confin'd" — mentally, morally, physically fettered—the mere instrument of a powerful hierarchy, a sheer despotism, which aimed to be in every country '*imperium in imperio.*' He endeavoured in vain to draw a satisfactory distinction between his spiritual allegiance to the Pope, and his temporal allegiance to England. If the Pope were merely a spiritual potentate, this might be possible—but the Pope is also a temporal prince; and as such his claims to the allegiance of the subjects of other countries must always be productive of misconception and vexation. The conclusion to which Father Stirling was gradually, but surely tending, was that (setting aside questions of pure Theology) the reformed religions were preferable in this; that they left more scope to the right of private judgment—and were consequently more consistent with the progress of science and human freedom.

But more than all advantages, in his present afflicted condition, did the thought press upon him, that had he been a priest of the

Reformed Religion, he might now have been a happy husband and father! How simple and easy to keep had the vow of perpetual celibacy seemed to him when he took it at twenty-four. It was, I believe, the young clergy who carried the vote for the celibacy of the priesthood. Can we wonder that the Catholic clergy, especially the aristocracy of the church, should be charged with ambition? The affections are starved. The heart remains undeveloped; but human nature must have some outlet. Human abilities must have some occupation. Is it any wonder that men so situated should grasp at honours and dignities? They must be unhappy whether they fulfil or break their vows of celibacy. This law of the church, first generally enforced by Gregory VII., in 1074, is at utter variance with the law of God written in the heart of man.

The assumption which enjoins celibacy on priests is that marriage is improper. The Roman Catholic Church appears to take a low and rather erroneous view of marriage. It is regarded as a mere physical necessity, not as an intellectual and spiritual longing. Yet Clement Stirling was an illustration that the mind suffered equally with the body. If there are saints who can so occupy themselves with prayers and religious meditations as to be entirely above the ordinary wants and wishes of humanity, Clement Stirling was not such. Yet was he a very good man. He may then be fairly considered as a type of the generality of suffering priests.* This living alone has a terribly depressing effect on the mind. The Rev. Father experienced an overpowering sense of solitude and *ennui*. It was not now as in the early days of his priesthood. Then, his parochial duties and works

* The clergy (good Catholics) of several parts of the south of Germany have formally expressed a wish that this disagreement should cease, and that the church should join the progress of the age which makes marriage the true modern state as celibacy was (at least ideally) that of the middle ages. The situation of the priest *alone*, yet not alone, free and not free, in the midst of a world in discord with him, reminds us of that of a man condemned to the cellular treatment, who should carry his cell about with him. Nothing would be more likely to make him mad. (See the four articles of Léon Faucher) Every one has read the late history of that Benedictine *Abbé* (I think in the Tyrol) who, not wishing to violate his vows, and not being able to be released from them, stabbed himself to the heart."—*Michelet.*

of supererogation, springing from a blind child-like faith, kept him constantly employed, with few moments for reflection. Now, he was considerably older; and despite his disinterestedness, he felt the very natural desire to live a little for himself. Science attracted and repelled him by turns like the opposite poles of a magnet. At one time, in its grand truths, he found consolation in thinking as *a man.* But the next came the consciousness that he was a priest of Rome! He shuddered at the recollection of his awful vows, at the sacrilege involved in their infraction, and at all which he had sworn to believe on the authority of the Church, so antagonistic to the teachings of science.

The reader cannot imagine this torture, but he may remember it. If he has once experienced it, indeed, he is not likely ever to forget it. To wish for action, to feel the absolute necessity of some engrossing employment to keep the mind from preying on itself, to prevent its possessor from becoming actually mad! To pass in review numerous congenial occupations, and to be able to practise none! To gaze listlessly on the manual of devotion which once held heart and soul entranced! To be unable to pray! To turn away shuddering from the glorious page of science as though it were some species of black art! Then the actual misery of being so much alone! To pass whole days without opening the lips; to lie awake in the silent watches of the night—to be the prey of an unmanly nervousness—to shrink at imaginary terrors—to long for a companion who would sympathise with and love him—to look forward to the still more cheerless future, the thought of growing old thus; then, in a desperate mood, to find a refuge in the images of fancy, to renew awake the visions of slumber, to indulge in dreams of domestic felicity—a loving wife, children, and home! When Father Stirling awoke from such dreams to the consciousness of the stern relentless reality, the reaction was so great that he trembled for his reason. His anguish was akin to that of The Opium-eater (though the experience was the reverse), when he exclaimed, "I will sleep no more." He would start wildly sometimes, and exclaim, "Am I alive, or does my soul already suffer the pains of hell?"

CHAPTER VI.

A GLEAM OF HOPE.

It was after a paroxysm of this mortal terror that he called again upon the doctor, who had already begun to usurp the place of confessor. Dr. Blunt did not conceal from his patient the critical condition of his health. "Doctor," said the priest, "tell me candidly. Hide nothing from me. Is not my reason in danger? Death I can face—but the loss of reason terrifies me."

"My dear sir," said the doctor, when Father Stirling had become somewhat calmer, owing to the effects of a soothing draught, "I will answer you candidly. I know of but one remedy. My experience enables me to go rapidly into the diagnosis of disease, both physical and mental. Indeed, the body and mind are so intimately connected that it is extremely rare to find diseases purely mental or purely physical. I have given your case particular attention. When you first came to me I own that, being in the dark as to your profession, I did not exactly grasp the full nature of your affliction. I thought it was a simple physical suffering, such as is common with men of your profession. But now I see clearly there is a psychological cause. Your disease is more mental than physical. There is at the bottom of your uneasiness something more than a mere longing to change your condition, to follow the example of men in general, to be a husband and a father." Here the doctor paused, and looked fixedly at the priest. Then, he added, abruptly, "I am very much mistaken if you have not formed an attachment?" A girl of sixteen could not have blushed more deeply than did Father Stirling. The doctor required no specific assurance that he had guessed aright. He went on quickly, without seeming to notice his patient's emotion.

"Your temperament is ardent—your heart is tender. To love is for you a peculiar necessity. This, then, is your position. You must choose between love and death. Vitality worn out will succumb sooner or later. Do not think I am saying this to frighten you. Nor do I pretend that the fatal termination may not be postponed by medical science. But this I do say—that if you persist in your present way of life you will never live to be old! Your conscientiousness is strong—to that I appeal. Why sacrifice yourself for an idea? Why throw away a good and valuable life? You are a priest. Be a priest still, but a priest of the reformed religion which permits her clergy to marry." The physician stopped, as if prepared for some strong opposition, but Father Stirling remained silent. The doctor continued:—

"It is, I trust, superfluous to say, that I am

speaking now merely as your medical adviser. I have no polemical interests to serve. To me Catholic and Protestant are alike. My own religious opinions I keep to myself. I have not time nor inclination to involve myself in theological bickerings. Let us have universal toleration, and let every man settle his religious conviction between himself and his Maker. In my eyes all religions are partly true, partly false. They are all emanations from the religious sentiment (which exists more or less in every human heart) diversified by natural local circumstances, such as climate, race, civilization. Burn all the theological books; sweep away every trace of religious worship in the world; and after a certain number of years more Bibles will be written; altars will again rise; sacrifices will be kindled; patriarchs and popes will pronounce creeds, issue decrees, and fulminate excommunications. You cannot extinguish religion in the heart of man, for man is a religious animal. Religion does not depend upon this or that language two or three thousand years old—that is, of yesterday, when compared with the age of the world and the antiquity of man. Religion preceded all languages! The first men worshipped God, and knew quite as much about immortality as men in the nineteenth century!

"I simply speak to you as a professional man. It is my duty to preserve life, and I know yours is a valuable life. Reflect on what I have said. You will not, of course, be able to look at it from my point of view. You will have religious scruples—your vows as a priest. But the obstacles arising from the difference between the Anglican and Roman Churches are surely not insurmountable. Both are Christian, and I am told that it is almost impossible to tell the difference between a Tractarian and a Roman divine. The only apparent difference is, that the Anglican clergyman may be a married man. You owe allegiance to Rome. But do you not owe duties to your country, to yourself, and it may be to another, or others? Conscience may suggest duties which may override those of ecclesiastical authority—aye, even of vows taken when you were an inexperienced young man. Of two evils choose the least. It is my duty to tell you plainly that you are doing violence to nature; that you are striving to annihilate a sentiment which is also from God. You need not renounce the clerical profession. You are a priest, but you are also a man, and an Englishman. Become a husband and a father, and you certainly will become a better priest. On the other hand, if you persevere in your present way, you are dooming yourself to certain death; you are morally guilty of suicide."

Father Stirling was too agitated to speak. He could only press the doctor's hand. The latter saw that further words were quite unnecessary. The priest hurried through the streets, eager to seek the silence of his own chamber, where he might reflect. His mind was a tumult. A gleam of hope had brightened the horizon of his gloom. The dream of happiness might become a reality. He saw himself restored to the privileges of manhood! Why should he not follow the physician's advice? His vivid imagination soared over all difficulties. He saw himself already blessed in the enjoyment of Madeline's love. He paced his room wrapt in a delicious transport. Suddenly his eye fell on Murillo's picture of the Virgin, and the current of his thoughts took a totally different direction.

What was it he was about to do? Abjure his allegiance as a Romish priest. Theoretically, nothing seemed more simple. He was an Englishman in England, a Protestant country. He would have the sympathy of the great majority of his countrymen. But by the Catholic party, those with whom he had lived and worked so many years—by them he would be regarded as a double renegade, a relapsed heretic. It is easy to talk of the power of the human will, the triumph of principle, and the free agency of man. But is man a free agent? Clement Stirling had nothing to do but to apply to a dignitary of the Anglican Church, and on making a solemn renunciation of the errors of Rome, he would have been admitted, without the necessity of fresh ordination, to the Anglican priesthood. But Clement Stirling was as incapable of doing this as though fettered in a dungeon of the Inquisition at Venice or Rome. Moral obligations, various and mingled motives, too minute and delicate for the gaze of the worldly spectator, bound him. As Gulliver in the hands of the Liliputians was mastered by an infinite number of pack-threads, each of which he could have snapped singly with a little finger, so was Father Stirling enclosed and overpowered by the meshes of tradition, of that strong fabric which Rome has industriously woven in centuries. He, an Englishman in London, a man of superior intellectual abilities, was morally the obedient humble servant of a foreign prince, an Italian priest, reigning in Rome.

How, after his apostacy, could he ever again bear to meet his Catholic friends and acquaintances? How could he support the burst of scorn and reproach, which (to the shame of our sham toleration) follows the man who asserts his right to think, and from conscientious motives changes his faith? Then, the Church—the church of his adoption—which he had served so faithfully; the grand old faith which he had professed for so many years, in whose ministry he had won such distinction, and known such spiritual happiness; how could he deliberately abjure its time-honoured doctrines—become guilty of the crime of sacrilege and dare the excommunication of God's Vice-gerent? Even if he dared all this for Madeline, how did he know that he would attain the prize? What if Madeline should refuse to wed a man who had apostatized from the Anglican and Roman faiths? What if Miss Winover's account were not exaggerated, and Madeline in everything but name were already a Catholic?

Such were the terrible revulsions of thought and feeling which agitated the unhappy priest!

CHAPTER VII.

JULIANA THE IRRESISTIBLE.

In the meantime, as may be imagined, Wiley was not idle. His vigilance did not sleep. Intimately acquainted with the sufferings of his friend, he thought it impossible that Father Stirling could longer resist temptation. The Jesuit knew well, from his own experience, the opportunities conferred on priests by the confessional and spiritual direction. He had been for some time anticipating that a venial error of this kind would be committed by Father Stirling. For, according to Liguori (a canonized saint of the Catholic Church), a priest is not bound to relinquish the duties of a confessor, because he falls occasionally. He had calculated the agony of conscience which would attend the fall of Father Stirling. Daily he had expected his friend to come and pour into his ear, under the seal of confession, the story of his frailty. The Jesuit would then have had in his power his penitent, whom he would have consoled and absolved under certain conditions. Even then, though he might not succeed in winning Father Stirling at once, he had faith in the adage—"*C'est le premier pas qui coûte.*" He believed that his eventual triumph was certain. But as time passed on, and no such confession took place, and as his emissaries employed to watch Father Stirling, brought no intelligence which warranted the supposition of any lapse from virtue, Father Wiley grew impatient. Father Monaghan, the *socius*, had also become almost intolerable. Some step must at once be taken to subject Father Stirling to the Jesuit's will.

For some time Father Wiley had been meditating a forlorn hope, to which he now determined to have recourse, not however without considerable reluctance. For the Jesuit actually loved the man whom he was endeavouring in such an unprincipled manner to circumvent. It is questionable how far any man is a free agent under the most favourable circumstances. Why, then, are men so eager to join secret societies, to become the units of systems which annihilate the slightest vestige of moral independence? Father Wiley was but the instrument of authority. He shuffled the responsibility from his own shoulders on to those of his superiors. He was obeying his vow of implicit obedience. The Jesuit then betook himself to an accomplice, who had hitherto never failed him in any piece of mischief in which her services were necessary. This accomplice was a beautiful and unprincipled woman. Juliana Wilder had been a dancer. Her mother had sold her to a nobleman when she was only sixteen. She was so extremely beautiful, both in face and figure, that she had been a favourite model with the celebrated painter E——y.

What contributed to render this woman especially dangerous was that, in addition to her remarkable personal attractions, she possessed great natural abilities, a tolerable education, and the most consummate hypocrisy. Gazing at her down-cast eyes, their violet hue shaded by her long eye-lashes, and the sweet air of modesty which played about her lips, a stranger would have taken her for some Perdita or Desdemona,—

> "A maiden never bold;
> Of spirit so still and quiet, that her motion
> Blush'd at herself;"

No one who saw her thus could have suspected that she was, instead, a wanton Cressida. Those whom she was bent on fascinating, deceiving, and betraying, hearing her speak in her gentle, silvery voice, with all the propriety of a virtuous woman, or sing after affecting the hesitation of a young lady in her first season, did not suspect that this woman was an accomplished actress, who could at a moment's notice, in the society of her familiars, resume her real character—so entirely opposite to her assumed manner and conversation.

From this cause the most opposite opinions were asserted of Juliana. While some called her the worst of women, the soul of vice, bad, vile, mercenary, without the excuse of passion for her sins; others defended her, eagerly declaring her to be the unfortunate victim of calumny and slander. With some she was a Lucretia: with others a Lucretia Borgia! Each spoke from sincere conviction. Each believed her to be what she seemed to him. Her attributes varied like the hues of the chameleon. She was reported to have said that she defied any man to resist her, if absolutely bent on captivating him.

This woman was only six and twenty. Yet she had already exhausted the experience of many lives. Though her heart was seared, her beauty had not suffered. She was tall and plump. Her figure was splendidly developed without being over-fleshy. She was like one of Sir Peter Lely's Hampton Court beauties. Various countries seemed to have combined their national traits to produce something near akin to perfection in physical charms. Her head was Greek; her bust was Austrian; her shoulders Italian; her foot Asiatic; her gait Andalusian; and her complexion English. Such was this woman, who only wanted one thing to be as attractive as she was dangerous—and that was virtue!

In one respect this woman was no hypocrite. She was not deficient in the religious sentiment. Exactly in proportion as she outraged the laws of God, and the principles of society, did she experience the necessity of some religious consolation. The little religious training she had received in youth was Catholic, and she had never abandoned the practice of confession. A good and earnest priest, by refusing absolution unless she abandoned her vicious career, would either have converted her or driven her away from confession altogether. But she fell into the hands of Father Wiley, who, seeing what a valuable instrument she might be made, set himself to mould her to his own purposes. In obedience to the principles of casuistry he had adopted from certain Jesuit doctors, Father Wiley calmed instead of awakening her conscience. He thought that if persons will sin, it is better they should be Catholic than Protestant sinners. Are the Jesuits the only people who act on this principle?

Thus Juliana pursued her profligate career, regular at confession, and wiping her sins off her conscience by periodical penances. By alternate gentleness and severity, the Jesuit maintained his power over his penitent, who served him with all the fidelity of a superstitious woman. It is not difficult to imagine that this famous (or infamous) member of the *demi-monde* could render very material services to the Jesuit. She possessed extraordinary influence over men holding a high position in society. Some would have beggared themselves or refused their own wives articles essential to their comfort, in order to gratify a whim of Juliana, who wielded her influence with discretion, and became possessed of important family secrets, which she communicated to Wiley. Left to her own guidance, Juliana would probably have married one of the good matches at her disposal, or, acting from mere temporary caprice, she would soon have converted friends into enemies. Led by the prudent counsel of her spiritual director, she succeeded in maintaining and consolidating her influence. She perceived the advantages which accrued to herself from this alliance; so that she was attached to the Jesuit by gratitude as well as by superstition. Moreover, though fond of money, she was not devoid of generous feelings. Once she pawned a diamond-ring, the gift of a duke, to relieve the necessities of a friend. Frequently she would use the superfluous wealth of some rich admirer to make a present to some poor suitor. She was a great contributor to religious charities, and always respectful and submissive to the priests. No wonder if they found it difficult to be harsh with her.

Such was the woman on whom Father Wiley confidently reckoned to procure the moral fall of Father Stirling. But even to such a woman as Juliana he found some difficulty in directly proposing his scheme. He had intentionally put her off on some excuse or other several times lately, when she came to confess; for this woman, living in sin, confessed regularly once a month, sometimes oftener, independently of the constant direction she received from Father Wiley. For three months he had refused to take her confession. One day, at the end of this period, he judged her sufficiently prepared for his purpose. She was in a tumult of apprehension. Her conscience was sorely overburthened, and she dreaded a severe penance. When she had finished, Father Wiley neither imposed a penance nor pronounced the usual form of absolution.

"You are angry with me, Father," said Juliana. "I know the catalogue of my sins is great, but you must remember I have not confessed for three months before. I know I did wrong to receive the visits of the banker, a married man with such a beautiful wife—I have seen her frequently; and they say she is as good as she is beautiful. But out of the check for two hundred pounds he sent me, (how like a banker, to make his first present in money! Lord Loosefish would have given me a bracelet or an India shawl), I gave twenty guineas to poor Henrietta, who was left utterly destitute by her lover. I contributed ten pounds to the Charity of the Little Sisters, and I have promised Father Dempster to purchase an altar piece of the Virgin he has set his heart on for his Chapel; nor have I ever failed daily to say *Pater Noster*, *Ave Maria*, and *Creedo.*"

"That is very well, daughter," said the

director. "You are young and beautiful. The pleasures of this world are not mortal sins if they be duly repented of, and if the sinner endeavours to make good overbalance bad works—and more than all, if the sinner has faith and obedience."

"Have I ever refused obedience, Father?" said the penitent, humbly.

"Not yet," said the Jesuit, "because perhaps in pity to your weakness I have hitherto exacted nothing which was extremely difficult of accomplishment. Do you not lead a pleasant life? Are you not famed as the possessor of beauty, wit, accomplishments? Have you not at your feet men whom the haughtiest women in the land covet?"

"That is perfectly true, Father," said Juliana, in a tone of gratified pride, for vanity was her besetting sin, and had been the cause of her ruin.

"And to whom do you owe this triumph? Who taught you how to conquer with method and to use your conquests with discretion?

Who, above all, affords you the consolation of religion; without which, you would be a poor lost impenitent sinner?"

"You, Father!" said Juliana, meekly. "Have I not shown myself deeply grateful to you for all your condescension, and for the spiritual comforts which I receive from you?"

"Listen to me, Juliana. I am disposed to make a further trial of your obedience. Hitherto, you have never failed under any trial. Are you prepared to undertake an extremely difficult affair, which will require all your valuable qualities to bring to a successful termination? Can I depend on you; or shall I seek another agent?"

Father Wiley said these latter words purposely to pique Juliana, by exciting jealousy. In reality, among several women who were his creatures, the Jesuit had selected Juliana, as the most beautiful, the cleverest, and, at the same time, the most unscrupulous.

"I listen, Father, quite ready to obey," replied Juliana, in a tone of resolution.

"There is a certain person, who must be exposed to the blandishments of beauty. Do you understand?"

"Quite," said Juliana, to whom this kind of service was by no means novel.

"But this person is no ordinary man. The affair will require great address, on your part."

"Hitherto, Father, you know that I have never failed with men high in station, and reputed *good*," replied Juliana, in a voice whose penitential tone ill concealed the exultation of her heart--for she had the same confidence in her beauty, that a pugilist has in his strength; a philosopher in his science; a general in his army. "Is this man a Duke or Prince?"

"He is much more than Duke or Prince; but it is not his worldly state I speak of. I refer to his moral worth. He is reputed to be a Saint."

"Ah," exclaimed Juliana, joyously. "What pleasure to vanquish a Saint! He will not be the first! Is he an old man?"

"His age is thirty-two."

"Handsome?"

"Comely, both in mind and person."

"Father, you greatly excite my curiosity to know who this person is."

"Bring him to your feet, Juliana, and I not only grant you absolution and indulgence, but I give you permission to marry this young man of fortune who has for the last year been sighing in your train; who offers you a position in society—an historical name, and a rent-roll of ten thousand a year."

"Father, your kindness overpowers me. Name the man I must bring to my feet. He is already vanquished."

"Father Stirling!"

"*Father Stirling?*" cried Juliana, in a tone of surprise and alarm.

"Father Stirling." A long silence followed.

"But, Father," began Juliana, in a faltering voice—"to tempt a priest to sin is sacrilege; and such a priest as Father Stirling is said to be by all ——"

"Ah," interrupted the Jesuit, in a tone of thunder. "Do you dare to rebel? Is this your vow of holy obedience? Is this your gratitude? I will employ another agent; and as for you, faithless woman, tremble lest I pronounce the irrevocable sentence of excommunication, which exiles you from the hope of pardon ——."

"Father, have mercy," cried the terrified Juliana. "I will obey in all things; but first give me absolution, and then promise me an indulgence for the grave sin of tempting so holy a man."

"I will not only absolve you, but I declare to you, that in tempting Father Stirling, you are committing no sin. It is for the Father's eternal welfare, that he should make one lapse from virtue, for in the words of Molinos, 'If the inferior part be without sin, the superior part grows proud—and pride is the greatest sin; consequently, the flesh ought to sin, in order that the soul may remain humble; sin producing humility becomes a ladder to ascend to heaven.' Is it not so with yourself, Juliana? Does not your sin render you humble and amenable to penance, and the consolations of religion? If you were not a sinner, you might resemble these Protestant ladies, who, trusting in their own virtue, laugh at confession. Will their good works save these wretched heretics?"

Juliana implicitly believed this teaching, to which she had become habituated. The sudden change in the Jesuit's manner, from ferocity to kindness, reassured her, and she promised to do her best to rescue Father Stirling from the consequences of pride, through the medium of a venial sin! Her director then pronounced absolution; after which he minutely instructed Juliana in the performance of her difficult part.

CHAPTER VIII.

JULIANA THE VANQUISHED.

The chief difficulty was for Juliana to gain access to Father Stirling. After meditating and rejecting many plans, the Jesuit hit upon the following expedient. He would attack Father Stirling through the medium of the confessional. In most Catholic Churches, it is customary for the doors to stand open, on other days of the week as well as on Sundays; and there are certain hours in which a penitent can always find a priest in the confessional. On the day after the conversation reported in last chapter, it was Father Stirling's turn to receive confessions. A lady dressed in deep mourning alighted from a carriage, at the door of the Church, and entered the confessional. The penitent proceeded to pour into the ears of the priest, a long and thrilling story; deeply affecting in itself, and also through the tears and sobs by which its relation was accompanied. The confessional is productive of profound sympathy. Father Stirling could not see his penitent, but there was only a plank between them. Her sweet and plaintive voice; her sighs and sobs; the rustle of her dress were plainly audible—these things, and the perfume emanating from her toilet, told him his penitent was a young and probably handsome woman.

Tears stood in the eyes of the confessor, as the tale of woe proceeded. It was unnecessary for him to interrupt by asking questions. The confession was made with a minuteness of detail, which brought the most vivid pictures before the mental vision of the priest—who was, indeed, rather inclined to check than encourage such a flow of words and impassioned description. The lady's story may be briefly told as follows. When a girl of seventeen, she had been married to a man of wealth and position in society. It was a marriage of convenience. She, a young girl, knowing nothing of the world or her own heart, had been, in a measure, forced to marry this man by her mother, an ambitious worldly woman. The victim felt no sentiments but those of indifference or aversion to her husband—who was a man old enough to be her father. The usual consequences resulted. A gentleman won the affections of the wife, and after a certain amount of solicitation she broke his marriage-vow.

Such was the story told with the most ingenious amplification by Juliana. It was a true and a trite story, only *she* was not the heroine of it. As far as it regarded Juliana, it was utterly false. The penitent stopped abruptly, apparently overwhelmed with grief. She had not finished her confession, but she declared that she could not remain longer at that time, without exciting her husband's suspicions. She begged permission to return and unburthen her soul, that she might receive penance and absolution, at the same hour to-morrow. Father Stirling said that, to-morrow, the confessional would be occupied by another priest. The lady replied, that she had come with the express purpose of confessing to the good Father Stirling, and to no other; and she prayed permission to finish her confession at the Rev. Father's private residence. Father Stirling replied that this was quite unusual; that he was not in the habit of receiving penitents at his house; but the lady seemed so eager and so unhappy as to the state of her soul, that the priest at length gave a reluctant consent.

Without recapitulating, the reader will bear in mind that this temptation came upon Father Stirling at a very critical period. There were moments, indeed, when, in the intensity of his agony, he despaired of everything, hope, virtue, and himself. A horrible fatality seemed to urge him towards the actual commission of a sin which he had already been compelled to dwell upon in thought. Then, too, the temptation approached him in such an insidious garb. In the exercise of his duties as confessor, he had listened to many stories, not dissimilar to that told by Juliana — revelations which would have quickened the pulse of an anchorite. In the present instance he was attacked through his weak points—sympathy and compassion for the sufferings of others. How could he be harsh to this woman's sin? She had been tempted, and had fallen. Did *he* not of all men know the cruel force of that universal passion, against which he had been told by the doctor that it was in vain to struggle? And the tempter whispered to him, "Why should you alone be virtuous?" Then he would fall on his knees and try to pray. But though his lips repeated the words, his thoughts wandered. In this terrible conflict he passed the day, waiting for the arrival of his penitent. The appointed hour came and passed, but the lady did not come. The priest felt a strange feeling of mingled disappointment and pleasure. Perhaps she would not come; perhaps the danger was past. Some instinct told him there was danger in this woman's visit; that he had not assented to such an unusual infraction of custom from perfectly pure motives; that her presence would be fraught with peril to him. His reason told him to be glad that she had not kept her appointment, and yet he could not feel glad. He was perfectly conscious of this extraordinary war of sentiment going on within his own heart; this duality of feeling, as though he possessed in himself two separate distinct identities.

At length, when the shades of night had fallen, a carriage drew up under the windows, and a knock was heard at the door of the priest's house. Old Hannah opened the door, and curtsied humbly to the visitor, whom she imagined to be some great lady. Nevertheless, in spite of Hannah's confidence in her master, her Scottish notions of propriety were greatly shocked by such an unusual occurrence as a visit from a lady, and in the evening, too. She preceded Juliana upstairs, and knocked at the door of the priest's apartment. Hearing no response, Hannah opened the door. This was the scene which was presented to the eyes of the two women.

Father Stirling was upon his knees before the picture of the Virgin. Evidently to the anguish of that day had succeeded some moments of spiritual calm. Wrapt either in contemplation of the picture or in some seraphic vision, the priest was too much absorbed to heed what was passing around him. He had not heard the low knock at the house door, or the light footsteps on the stair, or the gentle opening of the door of his room. He had, perhaps, forgotten all about his penitent. On the table stood a tray, containing his simple evening refreshment, untasted. The tea which Hannah had brought up as usual was quite cold. The housekeeper, seeing how her master was occupied, motioned to the lady to be seated, and departed, gently closing the door after her.

Juliana was not now dressed in mourning, but in a splendid evening costume. A crimson opera-cloak, worn over a dress of green satin, formed a rich contrast to her shining black hair, and the dazzling white of her magnificent shoulders. Among the rings she wore, sparkled a valuable diamond. Jewelled ornaments of an exquisite workmanship depended from her ears, and a bandeau of pearls encircled her brow. But the change in her external appearance was not greater than that going on within her heart. Juliana's emotion at the confessional on the previous day had not been altogether counterfeit. Her conscience was not so hardened under the direction of the Jesuit as to permit her to tell, unmoved, a tissue of falsehoods under the seal of confession. True, she had not seen Father

Stirling, but it must be remembered that his reputation had already inspired her with awe, and she had from time to time heard the sounds of his gentle compassionate voice; and that voice which faltered, and betrayed the impressions made by her confession, had touched her deeply. What was the compunction then felt, to what she now experienced?

She cast a glance around the apartment. She beheld the walls covered with common paper; the bare floor; the shabby furniture; the grate without a fire, although the weather was cold. How different was this from the abode of the Jesuit! How different from the luxury of her own apartments in Sloane-street. Lastly, her eyes dwelt upon the priest himself—the anchorite, the fitting occupant of such a cell. The light of a solitary lamp which hung from the ceiling, fell on his closely-cropped hair, and impigned here and there on his immovable figure, like the picture of a Spanish monk, after Velasquez or

Murillo. Juliana began to feel a strange sensation of awe rising in her heart. She was as we have seen superstitious; but now she began to experience a genuine alarm of conscience. She felt the terror of a guilty being, who had intruded on holy ground. Her first impulse was to creep away, to fly, without being seen by the priest, for she dreaded to meet his eye. But she remained stationary, afraid to move, almost afraid to breathe. It was terrible to be alone in the room with that silent motionless figure. It was a relief to her highly-wrought feelings, when she heard faint tones proceeding from the lips of the priest. For the first time during that day the evil genius seemed to have been vanquished. The priest seemed to have banished the recollection of his own sufferings in those of another. He was praying for his penitent, and by implication, for himself. He, who, years ago, would have visited such a confession with a severe penance, now taught by his own bitter experience, felt the impossibility of adequately discharging one of his priestly functions—that of *judge*! The conscience-stricken woman listened to an eloquent prayer on behalf of herself, ending with the sublime words of Jesus—"He that is without sin among you, let him first cast a stone at her."

Here the priest was startled by a prolonged sigh, and, turning round, he saw Juliana. He rose immediately and approached her. Juliana trembled greatly as she beheld, for the first time close at hand, this remarkable man; as she saw his noble countenance, furrowed with the traces of mental suffering; his stooping figure, worn and emaciated with fasting and maceration. How different from Father Wiley was this priest, and yet to this priest she had lied in the confessional! It was this man she had undertaken to make an accomplice in sin! Obeying an irresistible impulse, the Magdalen fell upon her knees before the priest, and hid her face in her hands.

Father Stirling, who saw in this action a fresh proof of remorse of conscience for the sin detailed the day previously in the confessional, stooped mechanically to raise her from the floor, but she shrank from his hand, exclaiming —

"Do not touch me; I am a great sinner."

"So are we all," said the priest, humbly.

"But I, Father—*I* am guilty of the crime of sacrilege. Everything I told you yesterday in the confessional was false."

The priest stared at her, as if he thought her mad. Juliana, with difficulty, checked the strong impulse which seized her to reveal all. She remembered that the Jesuit was even then waiting to learn the event of this interview; and the instinct of terror was too great.

"Father," she said, "pity me. What could induce me, a stranger, to act so diabolically? That is the question which you have a right to ask. That is what I would like to reveal. But I dare not. I acted upon moral compulsion, and I cannot explain the cause of my extraordinary conduct without implicating, and telling the secrets of another. Now, shall I speak, or be silent?"

"Be silent," replied the priest.

"What?" continued Juliana. "You do not insist upon knowing my motives for deceiving you—for telling so many abominable falsehoods, under the seal of confession?"

"You say," replied the priest, "that you acted under compulsion, and I believe you. You are to blame, but those who took advantage of you and forced you into the commission of this crime, are doubtless much more to blame. God knows your motives. To Him you must appeal for pardon."

Juliana's surprise and emotion became every instant greater. How different was this teaching from what she had heard from Father Wiley!

At this moment the colloquy was interrupted by Hannah, who entered hastily, with a letter which had just come by post. The letter was sealed with black wax, and on the back was written—"To be opened without a moment's delay." The handwriting was quite unknown to Father Stirling, but he obeyed the injunction on the back of the letter. No sooner had he read two or three lines than he staggered and turned pale. The letter stated that his mother was not expected to survive, and directed him, if he wished to receive her last farewell, to set out at once for his county-town.

END OF VOL. I.

CPSIA information can be obtained
at www.ICGtesting.com
Printed in the USA
LVHW101342160422
716387LV00003B/128

9 783752 593754